NONYELIM OKOLIE

STONE ORIGIN

HOW TO LIVE A LIFE GOVERNED BY DIVINE PRINCIPLES

NONYELIM OKOLIE

I

STONE ORIGIN

How to Live a Life Governed by Divine Principles

ISBN 978-978-973-216-6

Published by Stone Origin Enterprise

Copyright © 2020

All Scripture are quoted and paraphrased from the Bible:
The Message (MSG)
Good News Translation (GNT)
King James Bible (KJV)
Stone Origin Network

Website: www.stoneorigin.com

Facebook: Stone Origin Network

Instagram: @stoneorigin

Twitter: @stoneorigin

Hashtag #TheBookStoneOrigin

Phone: +234 812 016 2101

Please send your reviews to;

stoneoriginnetwork@gmail.com and tag us on social media.

Table of Content

Endorsements

Wow...the book, Stone Origin...is a book for every young person who wants to be relevant in God's agenda in the now. It's a very small handbook you can read in a few minutes but the nuggets inside it are so powerful they can impart & impact you forever. I am excited about this book, because we are in the times where young people need to take caution and live life the right way. I am convinced that anyone who picks this book will find it helpful. Amongst many options and questions in our times, I present to you, Stone Origin.

**Akin Akinpelu Consultant,
Trainer & Pastor**

Stone Origin is carefully written and packaged for young people. The author addresses the peculiar issues youths are grappling with and emphasizes on divine solutions to the major challenges of the day. It is a clarion call to youths to embrace and live by tried and tested divine principles.

Dr. D.K. Olukoya

General Overseer, MFM Worldwide

Stone Origin is a book full of practical wisdom on the very important aspects of life (purpose, relationships, work, studies, et cetera). It contains several life changing and thought provoking truths such as these: "Time spent judging others should be reinvested in self-development;" "Do not trade your joy for your desire;" and "There are blessings attached to following due process." It points people to God and encourages them to have a relationship with Him. Stone Origin reveals to youths the ultimate secret of success and happiness: to put God first and to love Him; to lean on Him, to live by His word and to work for Him. Every young person, single and married, should read this book! I would love to give every member of my church a copy. Nonye says that life is governed by divine principles, which is absolutely true; and she has shared those principles here. Anyone who reads this book and applies the principles shared will enjoy a successful, prosperous and happy life.

Chinaemerem Ibezim

Pastor, Able Ministers Chapel

This Book is targeted at youth readers. It is a good book to help them live a better life with relevant bible quotations.

O. Bank-Olemoh
Chairman, MFM Media Committee Worldwide

In a world largely distracted by #trends and trivialities, this book is a definite guide to addressing many life issues affecting the youth today. This book is an encyclopedia of life principles governed by divinity. You can never go astray applying the principles laid out in this book. A must read for every youth.

Emeka Nwarulor
Author, Stand Out or Get Lost.

How simple can a book be? It pricks the conscience, guides you and guards the intent, passes in clear language and still lifts you if gloomy. A short while being friends with Nonye proves pearls could still be found in dirt; this tells of your values and how gracious it is to share and impact your world. I highly recommend this wonderful piece. My advice to the readers - three things matter most...God, His word and genuine love for your fellow man.

Bruce Imoesi Imagwe
Team Lead, Welvarend Ltd

Stone Origin offers great guidance based upon Biblical standards. It has the capacity to probe, expose, encourage and change the reader. It has definitely left an indelible mark on my mind. Thus, if you want to get better at something, if you want to be successful, keep a pencil nearby. Trust me, you'll need it. Anyone who is interested in improving himself/ herself will most probably be interested in reading this book. Readers will gain very valuable knowledge on how to live a better, more fulfilled life using time-honoured principles. It touches on areas such as love, marriage, business, financial, management,leadership, and death.

Seun Lari-Williams

Lawyer, Poet and a Flutist

His book, "Garri for Breakfast" was longlisted for the NLNG prize for literature in 2017

Indeed, the story of a success or the success of a story is best told at the hilltop. The youth who has gone through life's high mountain and reaches the zenith can only do so with guidance of handling youthfulness, singlehood, courtship and marriage within the balance of scriptural knowledge and vision.

Funsho Olorunfemi
Lawyer, Writer and Humanitarian

Praise For The Author

Nonyelim Okolie is a strong voice in this generation. She is gentle, tender but also full of wisdom. The book STONE ORIGIN is a proof of how her life is evolving. She has a passion to see people transformed and live life the right way. Nonye, you are going somewhere to happen. This generation is grateful for the sacrifice of putting this together.

Akin Akinpelu
Consultant, Trainer & Pastor

Nonye is a true believer that has boldly declared her faith in God and in His word. Nonye hasn't only written from the Bible, she is living an exemplary life - she's cheerful, loving, compassionate, industrious, purposeful and passionate about life and whatever she does. Stone Origin establishes Nonye as a fantastic teacher and communicator; her writing is clear, accurate and straight to the point. Using her own words, Nonye is best described as a beautiful soul.

Chinaemerem Ibezim
Pastor, Able Ministers Chapel

Nonye is the real deal. Her passion for humanity, growth and development and being a formidable support for a cause she believes in is one worth emulating. She's a lady who is principled and I can see a reflection of who she is in this book.

Emeka Nwarulor
Author, Stand Out or Get Lost.
Founder, Big Brand Academy

Nonye deserves a lot of credit for making understanding easy for her readers. In an elegant, yet contemporary manner, she applied God's Word to today's world and our everyday life using relatable illustrations.

Seun Lari-Williams

Lawyer, Poet, Flutist and Author, Garri for Breakfast

Nonyelim Okolie carries a passion for helping her generation push beyond the boundaries of limitation. She could easily be part of those asked to spy the land and come back with the report that the land is filled with milk and honey rather than giants!
In our world filled with worrisome ideologies, propelled by digital wavelength of limitless information, a vista of disciplined instructors is a desideratum.

Nonye is part of those instructors, using her writings and forum to offer better direction, clearer focus and achiever-mentality among her generation. She believes direction is more important than speed and carries the flag of honour in leading others within the creeks of adulting.

Funsho Olorunfemi
Lawyer, Writer and Humanitarian

You Are Unstoppable!

To every millennial out there, wisdom is key and balance is necessary. We are in a fast- paced world where we run with the wind of the dog race. To build the future and be given your place, you need to have an edge over others in your generation. There are many things far better than money and fame in life...wisdom, good name, healthy relationships and all. Strive to preserve this leading through life. I believe in you guyz.

Akin Akinpelu

Consultant, Trainer & Pastor

We're living in one of the greatest times and the opportunities available for us are enormous. Unfortunately, there are also numerous distractions and temptations. However, a disciplined and determined youth will surely succeed. More and more people in our generation have no real relationship with God and some no longer believe in His existence: God exists and being our Maker; life without Him is meaningless. If you believe in yourself, nothing and no one would be able to stop you. There are challenges but they are surmountable. Look around you, young people all over the world are doing extraordinary things, breaking records and setting new ones and exceeding expectations: they are people just like you and I. Dream big! Dare to do the impossible. Choose to be great! Yes, you can. Yes, you will.

Chinaemerem Ibezim Pastor,

Able Ministers Chapel

To the youth, here is one classic advice, "To achieve greatness in any endeavour, delayed gratification must become a strategy."

Emeka Nwarulor

Author, Stand Out or Get Lost. Founder, Big Brand Academy.

Acknowledgements

Thank you, Lord, for your grace and unfailing love. I trust you for greater things. To Mrs Dorothy Okolie, my mother, who lived a disciplined life and taught me the way to go. To Mr Joseph Okolie, my Father, who ensured he gave me the best in life. To Chibueze Okolie and Chiwete Okolie, my brothers for being very caring and protective.

Thank you to Pastor Akin Akinpelu for spurring in me the urge to impact my generation. Thank you to Pastor Taiwo and Pastor Bank-Olemoh, words cannot express my gratitude to you for your professional advice and assistance towards this book. Thank you to Pastor Biodun Segun and Pastor Olaide Kunle for the values and knowledge shared with me at a very young age. Thank you to Dr. Daniel Olukoya for raising an army of spirit filled Christians. *The sermon, Dancers at the gate of Hell by Dr. Dk Olukoya is life transforming.*

To Samuel Ekpe, thanks for always believing in me. To James King, thank you for teaching me so much about the power of the mind and the love of God. To my Cousin, Dumebi Ojogwu and friends Tosin Shonaike, Chinonye Osuagwu, Adedeji Conde, Taiwo Akinwunmi, Adigun Olalekan, Dike Nwannaka, Dozie Igweilo, Innocent Udeogu, Ayobami Oyaleke, Owo-eye Monday, Opeyemi Owosho, Eyewuene Murphy- Akpieyi, Monica Ofagbe, thanks for the encouragement to proceed with this work and for offering your time and insight. Thanks Pastor Bank Olemo, Kolawole Segun, Emmanuel Adegboye, Funsho Olorunfemi and Mark Ahamefule for the book edits. I want to use this opportunity to say a big thanks to Hammed Goodman Okunade for the beautiful book cover, Bright Odionye and Ikechi Adolphus for the first and second iterations of the Stone Origin website.

To my mentors, Emmanuel Tarfa, Olufunbi Falayi, Taiwo Ajetunmobi, Mfon Ekpo, Chude Jideonwo, Adebola Williams, Bukonla Adebakin, Babajide Asegbeloyin, Olayinka Taiwo, Christopher Eshemokai, Remi Dairo, Jeffery Okolo, Oluwaseun Runsewe, Benjaminn Okpalo, Tayamika Mattao, Owolabi Williams, Dayo Israel, thank you for giving me an opportunity to learn, serve and impact lives.

Introduction

The most powerful book on earth is the Bible. All Scripture is inspired by God. Through Faith and adherence to God's word, your life can change drastically for good. Each Scripture quoted in this book is key to our understanding of the divine principles that govern our lives. God is calling every one of us into obedience so He can make use of us to depopulate the kingdom of darkness. Despite the rate of moral decadence in our society, I wish for every individual on earth to live a better life. I know this is possible through grace.

This book is universal. Individuals ought to discern between what is wrong from right and avert from taking negative decisions that would have dangerous consequences in future. Stone Origin would aid young people in having a very strong positive moral foundation in life, so that millennials would avoid making irreversible mistakes.

Live by divine principles, be the best you can possibly be and most importantly, develop a positive attitude. A positive attitude is a very potent source of happiness. Give thanks to God every second of your life. Do not be discouraged even when things don't go as planned. Challenges don't last forever. Always trust God in your struggle.

Personal Declaration

I encourage you to ask the Lord to grant you wisdom as you read this book and begin to live your best life.

Philippians 4:13 (AMP)
"I can do all things [which He has called me to do] through Him who strengthens and empowers me [to fulfill His purpose—I am self-sufficient in Christ's sufficiency; I am ready for anything and equal to anything through Him who infuses me with inner strength and confident peace.]"

• Thank you, Lord, for your endless love for me.
• Dear holy spirit, be my comforter, grant me divine wisdom, give me a deeper understanding of the life beyond and enable me to reach the peak of my spiritual progress in Christ; loving God wholeheartedly just as much as He loves me.
• The season for me to reflect God's glory has come; I shall live a life worthy of emulation.
• The decisions I take shall transform me to who God wants me to be.
• I have not come to this world in vain.

CHAPTER 1

God First

God is Omniscient; He has divine wisdom and knows the end from the beginning. God is Omnipresent, He is everywhere. God is Omnipotent; He has great power and influence. God created the heaven and the earth and your life must depict that purpose of God's sovereignty. God upholds all things and when you love God endlessly and put Him at the center of your life, every other thing in life would be taken care of. God created you and He alone deserves the glory. God's love is amazing and follows you even in the darkest periods of your life. Only God can love you in ways no man can. He'll fight for you and open doors no man can shut. Trust God and acknowledge Him in all your ways and He shall direct your path.

Matthew 6:33-34 (AMP)
"But first and most importantly seek (aim at,
strive after) His kingdom and His righteousness
[His way of doing and being right—the attitude
and character of God], and all these things
will be given to you also. So do not worry about
tomorrow; for tomorrow will worry about itself.
Each day has enough trouble of its own"

The Word of God is the most potent means God uses to talk to any man. All you have to do is to read, meditate and believe in His word. God will give you the strength to serve, learn and develop yourself. Acknowledge God while you're young; be eager to know Him and desperate to reflect His glory, so you can be free from the predominant world system. Life is too short to live by chance.

NAOMI

Naomi is a young girl with big dreams and audacious goals, whose ultimate goal in life is to make heaven. She strives each day to live a Christ like life. She isn't perfect, just like you and me and had so many struggles. After she gave her life to Christ, she handed all her worries and concerns to God and accepted that His grace will be sufficient to help her, especially in those moments she couldn't help herself.

God's interest is in the souls of men and He is interested in living inside of us, only if we let Him. Let go and let God. Let go of anything that steals your joy and peace of mind, forgive freely and be at peace with everyone, irrespective of how much you have been hurt. I know this can be very difficult but it is also possible.

1 Corinthians 15:58 (MSG)
"Throw yourselves into the work of the God, confident that nothing you do for him is a waste of time or effort."

In her quest to please the Master, Naomi started working selflessly in her local church. She realized that being useful in His vineyard has a lot of blessings attached to it. She began to know the mind of God and at His appointed time He began to grant her the desires of her heart; she got the admission she had prayed for and was surprised at how her school fee was raised.

You see, nothing you do for God is a waste of time; be it evangelism, choir ministration, giving of alms, cleaning the house of God or ushering. Whenever you work for God, be rest assured, He will make things work for you. Your gift should be used to serve God.

Deuteronomy 10:12-22 (MSG)
"So now Israel, what do you think God expects from
you? Just this: Live in his presence in holy reverence,
follow the road he sets out for you, love him, serve
GOD, your God, with everything you have in you,
obey the commandments and regulations of GOD
that I'm commanding you today—live a good life"

Life is governed by divine principles and to excel in life, you can't afford to be careless. Obey God and live a good life. Do not get so preoccupied with the activities of the world and forget the one thing which matter most.

Matthew 6:24 (KJV)
"No man can serve two masters: for either he
will hate the one, and love the other; or else he
will hold to the one, and despise the other.
Ye cannot serve God and mammon."

The spirit realm is more real than the physical realm. Follow divine principles; do not focus on only what you want, which may lead to the detriment of your salvation and relationship with God.

OLIVER

Oliver was a young man, who was raised in a Christian home. He was very anxious for wealth. He was always intimidated by his peers who were driving cars and footing the bills at alumni events and social hangouts. He wanted to be like them, so he confided in one of them who introduced him to diabolical means of making money. He became trapped in the act of idolatry. He made some money doing it but he had no joy. He knew the source of his fortune wasn't genuine and he wasn't proud of it either but he allowed the pursuit of wealth lead him to sin.

At a point, he wanted to back out but his life was threatened.

They had told him that if he backs out, he will die and he had gone so deep into sin; it seemed difficult to come out of it. He was scared of dying or becoming poor. Fortunately for him, he has a loving family, who always prays for him. Eventually, he came out of it because he confided in his family and was saved. God ministered to him by himself and he surrendered his life to God. He discovered that it's only God that makes a man rich and adds no sorrow to it.

A man cannot be diabolical and claim to serve the living God at the same time. Do not consult fetish powers or take charms, oaths, incisions, and covenants in a quest for riches or for protection. There is no free gift from Satan. When the devil gives, what he takes back will always be far greater than whatever he will give. If you love God, you have no business with the evil one, even when you're enticed with temporary and vain things. You must remain patient and you put your trust in God.

A gift from Satan is an exchange for one's soul. It's a temporal relief in exchange for a lifetime of pain. Only God's grace can turn any situation around for good. We came to this world with nothing and we would all leave with nothing. While on earth, be yourself, pursue a righteous life: a life of faith and love. If a man lusts desperately after money or material gains, he may end up in trouble and live a life of regret. Trust God for genuine wealth.

Ecclesiastes 12:13 (MSG)
"Fear God, and keep his commandments;
for this is the whole duty of man"

All God wants from you is your total obedience. You are on earth to glorify Him. When you obey Him, you become an instrument for Him and your life would draw others closer to Him. Walking with God requires total obedience.

If you want God's protection, you need to fear God and avoid sin. Secret sin kills gradually. The fear of God would deter you from doing anything contrary to His will. Love God, love yourself and love your fellow man.

Hebrews 7:19 (KJV)
"For the law made nothing perfect, but the bringing in of a better hope did; by the which we draw nigh unto God."

Christ loves us and gave himself for us. Galatians 2:16-21 stated that man isn't justified by the works of the law but by faith in Jesus Christ. Do not frustrate the grace of God; righteousness does not come by the law but by grace through faith. Just believe in Christ and you are saved.

1 Corinthians 12:9 (KJV)
"And he said unto me, My grace is sufficient for thee: for my strength is made perfect in weakness. Most gladly, therefore, will I rather glory in my infirmities, that the power of Christ may rest upon me."

God expects you to depend on Him for everything. For any challenge in life, God has made a provision for you to overcome. God has given you all you need to have your needs met. Whatever situation you find yourself, it's to make you a better person. Christ will give you the grace to overcome.

Decision Exercise:

....

....

....

....

....

CHAPTER 2

A LIFE OF PRINCIPLES

The word of God in Exodus 20:1-17 states that we should not worship any other God except the Lord God Almighty, the Creator of the universe. Do not curse your fellow man using God's name. Observe the Sabbath day: refrain from personal activities that hinder you from being in God's presence. You ought to be grateful to God for keeping you alive till this day. Honour your parents: they brought you into this world. Do not kill: no one except God has the power to create life, so if no man can create life, no one should terminate a life. Do not sleep with anyone you are not married to. Do not take what does not belong to you. Avoid lies and gossip. Be satisfied with what God has blessed you with and do not be covetous; stay focused and ignore distractions. Obedience to the law, as stated in the Holy book, should be as a result of love and not fear.

Romans 13:9-10 (GNT)
"The commandments "Do not commit adultery; do not commit murder; do not steal; do not desire what belongs to someone else"— all these, and any others besides, are summed up in the one command, "Love your neighbour as you love yourself." If you love someone, you will never do them wrong; to love, then, is to obey the whole Law."

Obeying the laws doesn't make you a perfect man; it draws you closer to God. No man is perfect but we must make conscious effort to be Christ-like. Hebrews 7:15-19 states that Jesus died for our sins; the resurrection power of God through His Son,

Jesus Christ has redeemed us. Grace is all you need. The law guides you in all truth; to lead and show you the way to go.

The Principle of Self Love

The first step to enjoying life is to love yourself. Love yourself without resentment. Self- love is the most important form of love. Don't wish to be endowed with the physical features of some other person before you can be confident in yourself. God created you in His image and likeness. You do not necessarily need to alter any of your body organs just to feel happy and confident about yourself.

PAMELA

Pamela was a dark-skinned lady. She was a true description of an ebony lady. She gained admission into a prestigious university and made new friends. A few years down the line, while in school, some of her friends began to make her feel her complexion wasn't seeking enough attention. She then decided to lighten her skin tone. She was introduced to a beauty expert who mixed some substances and guided her through the application process. One month after she started applying the cream, she was getting compliments and admiration. Her skin colour popped and she was lighter.

She really enjoyed the attention, so she kept using the substance, even more than what was prescribed to her. After a period of time, people began to bring to her attention some discolorations in certain areas of her body. She suddenly realized the chemicals were not doing her any good. She stopped applying the cream and started using shea butter, which rejuvenated her skin to an extent.

Beauty goes beyond the colour of your skin. If you feel you're beautiful, then you are. Don't compare your physical appearance with others. Rather than dwell on your looks, develop yourself to the point where you are described as a person with a beautiful soul. You can't get the world to love and admire you if you don't love yourself.

The Principle of Self Development

No one is perfect; let your positives be more obvious than your imperfections. Don't focus
on your external beauty, develop your inner qualities.

Learn to know yourself more each day you're alive; understand your temperament and your personality. How you feel determines how you think of yourself, your worth, confidence and attitude towards people, which will, in turn, determine how others see you. Always invest in personal development. Understand your purpose and act towards being the best you can be. Be conscious of your health, exercise as often as you can and eat healthily. What you feed your physical body determines how your physical body looks just like what you feed your spirit man reflects in your spiritual growth.

The Principle of Gratitude

You are very important! Never look down on yourself or envy anybody. Be grateful for where you are and have faith in God. Be faithful in all you do, even when no man is watching. Have patience and persevere, very soon the grace you carry would become obvious to the world. Do not engage in unhealthy comparison. Take an inventory of your life and compare it with what God would have you do. Don't compare your progress in life with some other person's progress in life. Draw close to God and He would reveal what your assignment on earth is. While fulfilling your purpose, you would have no time to compare yourself to others or use their achievement as a yardstick to weigh the quality of your life.

Everyone has their stories; everyone's chapters are different. God knows what He gave you and God created everyone in His image and likeness. Don't compare others either, it isn't wise. Don't compare your spouse, don't compare your parents and don't compare your children. Instead of hurtful comparison, cheer them up, encourage them to be the best they can possibly be, let them see God in you. Instead, encourage them to draw closer to God.

Proverbs 23:17-18 (GNT)

"Don't be envious of sinful people; let reverence for the Lord be the concern of your life. If it is, you have a bright future."

Comparison produces bitterness and it's unhealthy for the soul. Rather than comparing yourself with others, focus on and enjoy the journey. The devil came and his sole purpose is to steal, kill and destroy. We live in a world where so many deep things happen. The desperation to get rich, the desire to get married, the urge to pass examinations, the quest for fame and power, among other earthly desires, has lured many into desperate acts like money rituals, fornication, adultery, prostitution and idolatry.

No matter what stage of life you are currently in, today you are laying the foundation upon which you must later live. God way is different from man's ways. To abide by God's standards at all times is paramount to our spiritual growth and our standing with God.

Mark 8:36 (MSG)

"What good would it do to get everything you want and lose you, the real you? What could you ever trade your soul for?"

Life is not all sunlight and roses for anyone. Just look at the bright side of life and in all situations, choose joy. Don't relent on doing well. At the right time, you'll reap what you've sown, if you persevere and not quit. The love of money also has led many people to make drastic negative choices just to amass material possessions that would eventually perish.

1 John 2: 15-17 (MSG)
"Don't love the world's ways. Don't love the world's
goods. Love of the world squeezes out love for the Father.
Practically everything that goes on in the world—
wanting your own way, wanting everything for yourself,
wanting to appear important— has nothing to do with
the Father. It just isolates you from him. The world and
all its wanting, wanting, wanting is on the way out—
but whoever does what God wants is set for eternity."

Always listen to the voice of God. Never listen to the voice of the evil one tempting you to do things contrary to God's purpose for your life. At times you might be tempted to compare your life with others. It's not necessary, focus on eternity.

Proverbs 17:22 (GNT)
"Being cheerful keeps you healthy. It is slow
death to be gloomy all the time."

Be happy; let nothing steal your joy. Don't let your present situation give you concerns.
Do not trade your joy for your desire. Don't hurt those you love by your actions today.

The Principle of Loyalty

Loyalty is a prerequisite for greatness. Life is synonymous with farming; you carry seeds but only you can determine which seed and how you intend to sow. Don't eat your seed; you might have nothing to reap. There is a time and season for everything on earth. Be diligent at what you do, determine what you want from the beginning and work hard towards achieving that goal. Be faithful in handling someone's business. In life, what you sow is what you reap. As an employee, be diligent at your work, understand the company goals, believe in the vision, work hard and contribute towards achieving the organizational goals. Never talk ill about those in authority; your management and always look out for the best interest for the organization.

Colossians 3:23-25 (MSG)
"Servants, do what you're told by your earthly masters.
And don't just do the minimum that will get you by.
Do your best. Work from the heart for your real Master,
for God, confident that you'll get paid in full when you
come into your inheritance. Keep in mind always that
the ultimate Master you're serving is Christ. The sullen
servant who does shoddy work will be held responsible.
Being a follower of Jesus doesn't cover up bad work"

Life is a battlefield and most times, those who survive are those who understand how the world operates. God can give you ideas that man cannot comprehend. It's left for you to take action and implement those ideas immediately. If you are faithful in what you do, God will bless the work of your hands. Use your gift well and it will bring you before great men.

Proverbs 14:22-23 (GNT)
"You will earn the trust and respect of others if
you work for good; if you work for evil, you are
making a mistake. Work and you will earn a living;
if you sit around talking you will be poor"

The Principle of Hard Work

Generate positive business ideas based on your hobbies and interests; what you see in the media, using valuable resources and materials. Be able to convert a vague idea into a viable business. It's only you who can use your ability with dexterity. Taking action gives you an opportunity to be who you want to be in life. Doing what you love would attract financial success eventually. Don't be skeptical about starting a business due to the unavailability of capital. In life, you shouldn't wait for things to happen to you. You need to have audacious goals. Take action to make it a reality and make a difference in your community.

Be passionate. Believe in your idea. Believe the business will succeed. Identify a need, a gap to be filled, conduct an in-depth research, build a product or a service and ensure you have a sustainable business model. When you solve a human problem, you'll be paid for it.

Get started and bootstrap using your savings to grow your business. As time goes by, you can raise seed capital from friends and family that trust you enough to invest in your business. Ensure your product or service has a perfect market fit. Develop a good prototype to attract external funding from seed investors, venture capitalists or for crowdfunding purpose. Make sure you know your data and your numbers.

When you take a business decision and it fails, rather than dwell on the situation or give up, think of how to fix it – go back to the strategy table. Life is all about taking calculated risks and in situations whereby you make a decision and it doesn't turn out as planned, it is an opportunity to learn and also prepare yourself for more calculative steps in your business, career and in life.

Have a defined goal that fits into your vision, set appropriate expectations, create the necessary structure and evaluate your successes and failures. There are great lessons to take away from failures. Failures could be a stepping stone to greatness. Resilience can't be developed in your comfort zone. Start that business today! In your community, identify the need or the problem, proffer solutions, and then turn it into a scalable business. People pay for value, not just the product.

Proverbs 20:19 (GNT)
"If you are lazy, you will meet difficulty everywhere,
but if you are honest, you will have no trouble"

Avoid idleness and seek to discover who you are, so that you can achieve more in life. The waiting period is crucial. It's really not about how long you wait but what you do while waiting. Don't be afraid, just do that which you have to do, continue to work hard, it will pay off eventually. Do not work for money, work to build the right relationships and impact in your community.

STEPHEN

Stephen was jobless for 19 years after graduation. He stayed at home blaming the government and his parents for not having the right networks to get him a job. He blamed himself for studying what he considered a "wrong course". He kept lamenting till the night he thought to himself, "I am not getting younger. I need to stop blaming others, take responsibilities and get myself out of this mess". He knew he was passionate about repairing gadgets. He decided to learn how to repair gadgets at computer village and after learning, he started a business. He started small, got so many clients and kept getting referrals since he was prompt to deliver and did a great job. His business boomed and he opened several service centers in Lagos and outside the city. He expanded the scope of his business and was a specialist in technology devices. He had so much money and decided to develop his intellectual horizon. He also learnt programming and is presently well sought after; he builds software for multinationals.

Stephen's life changed for good because he took a step and he wasn't complacent in his life's journey. He stopped blaming others for his failures and acquired the necessary knowledge and skill in line with what he was passionate about.

Proverbs 16:1-3 (GNT)
"We may make our plans, but God has the
last word. You may think everything
you do is right, but the LORD judges your motives.
Ask the LORD to bless your
plans, and you will be successful in carrying them out"

Don't wait for opportunities, seize the moment and make the best out of life. Take advantage of where you are and what God has blessed you with. Don't just wish to succeed in life, take action steps towards that idea God has been laying in your heart and don't neglect the power of starting small. To succeed in life, put God first, have a vision, work hard, be creative, avoid procrastination and be contented. Then avoid bad debt and greed.

The Principle of Giving

Giving multiplies all that you have and the word of God says, "It is more blessed to give than to receive". You honour God by giving to others and by taking a significant portion of what He has blessed you with to the church. The church means several things to several people. To some, it's the presence of God; to some it's a place of solace, to some it's a place of worship, to some a gathering of believers. I have come to an understanding that the church is not the building; the church is the body of Christ; the people.

Proverbs 3:9-10 (KJV)
"Honour the Lord with thy substance, and with the first fruits of all thine increase: So shall thy barns be filled with plenty, and thy presses shall burst out with new wine."

To be purpose-filled, it's necessary to live a selfless life. Selflessness is a priceless possession. Giving without expecting anything in return gives fulfillment and this attitude can take an individual far in life. When your selfless attitude is felt in the life of man, it serves as a legacy. God encourages us to give sacrificially. Give that which God has blessed you with; your time, knowledge, money and everything else.

Malachi 3:10-11 (KJV)
"Bring ye all the tithes into the storehouse, that there may be meat in mine house, and prove me now herewith, saith the Lord of hosts, if I will not open you the windows of heaven, and pour you out a blessing, that there shall not be room enough to receive it. And I will rebuke the devourer for your sakes, and he shall not destroy the fruits

*of your ground; neither shall your vine cast her fruit
before the time in the field, saith the Lord of hosts."*

God wants to bless those who are obedient, generous, kind, faithful and with a giving spirit. A tithe is 10% of all God has blessed you with. You could decide to give more, if led by the Spirit. God is not interested in spending your tithe. All God wants is your total obedience, not to question if the Pastor is the one who takes the money or not. When you tithe, God promised in His word that He would bless you abundantly; rebuke the devourer for your sake. Devourer could be accidents, sickness until death, failures at the edge of a breakthrough and some issues of life. I learnt years ago from my mother that when you pay your tithe, things would never be tight for you. Even if you have little, God would make it sufficient for you and He would always meet you at the point of your need.

Luke 6:38 (GNT)
*"Give to others, and God will give to you. Indeed, you will
receive a full measure, a generous helping, poured into
your hands—all that you can hold. The measure you
use for others is the one that God will use for you."*

Giving propels multiplication. Do not be compelled or reluctant to give. All your focus ought to be on obeying God's command as regards giving and the God who sees what you do in secret would reward you openly. The voice of God would not question your giving. Ensure your thoughts are always good. Do not listen to the voice of the devil and question who takes the tithe and what it is being used for. Judge no man, obey God and do what you ought to do.

Decision Exercise:

....

....

....

....

....

CHAPTER 3

A LIFE OF PURPOSE

The ultimate purpose of man on earth is to glorify God, to be faithful to Him and to live a life of service. Purpose gives life a meaning, focus and direction. When an individual understands this, life becomes more purposeful. Purpose also creates true happiness and a feeling of being part of something greater. It's only God that can fill you with divine purpose.

Ecclesiastes 9:9-10 (MSG)
"Each day is God's gift. It's all you get in exchange for the hard work of staying alive. Make the most of each one! Whatever turns up, grab it and do it. And heartily! This is your last and only chance at it, For there's neither work to do nor thoughts to think In the company of the dead, where you're most certainly headed."

When your purpose is not known, you'll be susceptible and there is a high chance you'll misuse opportunities and your time on earth. So, as long as you are on planet earth, there's a reason for your existence. Life is short and death is inevitable but while living, be the best version of you there can ever be. Purpose sometimes can be that thing which you are doing right now. Find purpose even in times of pain and discomfort - all things will fall in place.

2 Corinthians 4: 5-6 (MSG)
"Remember, our Message is not about ourselves; we're proclaiming Jesus Christ, the Master. All we are is messengers, errand runners from Jesus for you. It started

when God said, "Light up the darkness!" and our lives
filled up with light as we saw and understood God in
the face of Christ, all bright and beautiful".

God created you for His purpose and you have to be connected with Him through grace to enable you to know His plans for you and what He'll have you do. In life, to live according to purpose, you cannot serve God on your own terms. Your journey through life should be purposeful and your life should be a reflection of Christ.

Purpose sometimes is what you say it is. Missions are the important things you need to do to accomplish purpose. Be disciplined and prioritize your activities; knowing that you create the life you want by your actions today. Your relationship and connectedness with God, your divine purpose, career and marital bliss (all things being equal) should be your
life's utmost priority. All you need to do is to trust God through the process; it may tarry but wait on God. The devil wants nothing more than for you to miss fulfilling your purpose. Live a life that cannot be interrupted by sin and accusations from the devil. To fulfill your purpose, you must be Christ-like. When you do not know who you are, the devil would make you what you're not. Pray until you fulfill your purpose and even while you're executing it.

Ecclesiastes 3:1 (MSG)
"There's an opportune time to do things,
a right time for everything
on the earth"

Life is in stages and measured most times by milestones and accomplishment in every facet. Trust God's timing and be happy in every phase of your life. Purpose is when you do what God wants you to do. You need to have a relationship with God so He can direct your ways. Be open-minded and enjoy your journey. Do not let people, money, situations and actualizations determine your joy.

Be happy irrespective.

James 1:5-6 (MSG)
" If you don't know what you're doing,
pray to the Father. He
loves to help. You'll get his help, and won't be
condescended to when you ask for
it. Ask boldly, believingly, without a second thought"

God in His Word has prescribed a way to live and He expects us to live by it and not by the world systems. God is not interested in those who feel they can help themselves. He is not keen on those who feel they don't need Him to become all they could be.

You can be anything you choose to be. It all starts in the mind. Our lives, most times, are a result of our thoughts. Think big, act big, be big and most importantly, believe in yourself. Your life is shaped by your thoughts. You can become great if you put your mind to achieving greatness. Your mindset is a very powerful tool for achieving greatness.

Proverbs 20:18 (MSG)
"Form your purpose by asking for counsel, then
carry it out using all the help you can get".

You are a solution to a problem. Don't be a problem to be solved. Develop your capacity to the extent of providing answers to some of life's daunting questions. Ask questions, conduct in-depth research, act on your ideas and eventually, you'll figure out what you were born to do. Set goals, get a mission and take charge of your destiny. You don't need to be perfect, just ensure you're moving towards a positive direction.

1 Peter 3:10-12 (GNT)
"'As the scripture says, "If you want to enjoy life and wish
to see good times, you must keep from speaking evil and
stop telling lies. You must turn away from evil and do good;

you must strive for peace with all your heart. For the Lord watches over the righteous and listens to their prayers, but he opposes those who do evil."

Your character and attitude towards your fellow human would have a significant impact on your journey through life. Be careful of the words you let out of your mouth. Do not speak ill of anyone, avoid gossip (negative discussions about people) at all cost and resist circumstances that will make you tell a lie. Tell the truth at all times.

Jeremiah 1:5 (MSG)
"Before I shaped you in the womb, I knew all about you. Before you saw the light of day, I had holy plans for you: A prophet to the nations— that's what I had in mind for you."

So many times, as humans, we fail to wait on God; we fail to seek His face to know His plans for us. God is aware of your desires. He'll take care of you. He'll never abandon you. He will give you the future you hoped for. God's wish is that you prosper.

God reveals himself to His children in several ways. It could be through dreams, visions, trance, prophecies, His word (Bible), a discerning spirit, speaking in tongues, the gift of interpretation, conscience among others. Discern whatever revelations you get to determine if it's of God or the devil. Even if it glorifies God or comes from the Scriptures or so far it's from the tempter, reject it.
As much as you want to succeed in life, never feel self-sufficient. In life, despite how hard you work, it's only God that can determine the outcome. Put God first, work smart and then work hard.

John 15:5 (KJV)
"I am the vine; you are the branches. If you remain in me and I in you, you will bear much fruit; apart from me you can do nothing. "

Success in life is achievable if you put your mind to it and you put your trust in God. You can change the world and achieve whatever you set out to do. In a quest to fulfilling your destiny, the greatest joy is in doing something in line with the reason you were created. Every man on earth is created for a purpose and you need to be close to God to discern your divine assignment: whatever God has called you to do. Also, you were born to make the world a better place.

Sirach 40:1 (GNT)
"Every person has been given a great deal of work to do. A heavy burden lies on all of us from the day of our birth until the day we go back to the earth, the mother of us all."

If truly you want to succeed in life, avoid procrastinating things that will add value to your life. Take your destiny in your hand and be the best you can possibly be. Always aim for the top and never give up on yourself. Believe in yourself and what you are capable of doing. Be value driven; know who you are by putting into practice things you are passionate about and you love.

Education is important and it gives one some advantage in life. Though education is not the only prerequisite for success, it's a necessity. In addition to getting a formal education, explore the informal education and learn valuable skills to enable you provide value that is necessary in the workplace and in the world.

Acquiring the right knowledge can never be a waste of time. Never take for granted an opportunity to learn, expand your intellectual horizon and mental capabilities, it would be useful eventually. Always do the right things at the right time. While in school, ensure you give your best and focus. This could help boost your pace in life and would give your parents or guardian joy on the successful accomplishment of a milestone they deem important.

Dr. D.K Olukoya once mentioned that "In life, you need to read if you want to escape from poverty". Your career can be tied to your ambition, so while selecting a course to study in the tertiary institution, ensure you have a long-term goal with that choice and if you find yourself studying a course you never wanted, pray and make good use of the opportunity. On the side, do that which you're passionate about but ensure it doesn't affect your grades in school. What is worth doing at all is worth doing well. Many young people take for granted the opportunity to be in the confines of a tertiary education. Some join sects and some others party till they are out of school.

The quest for an active social life has prevented a significant number of undergraduates from graduating with good enough grades or at the set time. A typical balanced life should encapsulate a healthy spiritual life, good education and a clear sense of purpose.

As a student, read as often as possible, attend lectures, submit all term papers, learn from brilliant minds and be respectful to everyone in your environment. Set your goals and strategize on how to survive in school from day one. Never misplace your priority.

Decision Exercise:

....

....

....

....

....

CHAPTER 4
WHILE SINGLE, BE SENSIBLE

Life is in stages. Never make yourself vulnerable as a result of the desperation to get married. Be happy with or without a spouse. While waiting for your significant other, develop yourself to be better. Trust God and don't try to work it out on your own. Listen to the voice of God and He'll guide your every step.

Relationships should be about helping each other grow become the best version you can both be and not about selfish motives. It is about helping each other get what you want as individuals and as a couple. You need to be with someone who inspires you and wants you to be better.

As a man, you can't live a scattered life and expect to attract a woman who is organized. When you become organized and decent, you attract the spouse God has in mind for you. You cannot fix your spouse neither is your spouse supposed to fix you. No one has the ability to fix anyone, only God. All you need to do is pray for yourself and intercede for your partner.

Marriage is God's remedy against the sin of fornication, to accomplish missions and for procreation. A healthy courtship is a foundation for a successful marriage. Avoid cohabitation; ensure you go through the right marital process before moving into your partners' house to make it a home. Ensure the dowry is paid, have a legal marriage and ensure a minister of God declares you man and wife.

NAOMI & NATHAN
Naomi loves adventure. During her stay in a foreign land, she fell

in love with Nathan. Nathan told her he was single and lived in an apartment of his own. He buys her gifts and gives her money. Naomi, being a young woman who had just completed her tertiary education; believed it was time to settle down. She felt indebted to him for his kindness and always tried to reciprocate. She was always visiting him and occasionally slept in his house. Sleeping in his house was an invitation to danger but Naomi didn't take cognizance of it. She cooked his meals, washed his clothes, cleaned the house and sleeps on the same bed with him at night. She did all she could do to make the relationship result in marriage but to no avail.

After a year, Nathan broke the news of his engagement to marry his girlfriend of 12 years. He had given his word to her and didn't want to disappoint her. Naomi wasn't surprised; she has experienced this with several men. Naomi was indifferent, she learnt some time ago that,

> **"What you compromise to keep, you might eventually end up losing it"**

She knew she couldn't use sex to trap a man. If she gives her body to a man who hasn't married her, she might lose her mind. She remembered nights where she had to struggle with him to avoid having sex with him when he really needed it. She remembered the pain she felt in her joints as a result of those struggles. She remembered she was tempted to satisfy her benefactor but didn't want to grieve her spirit. She chose to be faithful to God's word even when her flesh was willing to sin.

There are blessings attached to following due process. During the period of waiting, your peers and acquaintances might describe you as being naïve; they may call you uptight and selfish. Just ignore those negative comments. Have it in mind that you are keeping yourself pure, not to please any man, but in reverence to God.

The process of being single, getting married and staying married has several challenges. What you do while single; your values, actions, learnings and mistakes will make a tremendous impact on your marital life. You really don't need to bother yourself about who your spouse is going to be. God has reserved the most amazing spouse on earth for you but before he finds you and before you make your intentions known to her, you need to concentrate on your priorities, which is your relationship with God who created you. Your assignment on earth and how you can impact your world without financial constraints or lack of insight is important. So, go ahead and develop yourself daily and make sure you're working in line with divine purpose before your marital breakthrough.

The courtship period should not be for the sole purpose of testing your partner's ability in bed or ability to cook. Courtship is a period where couples get to know each other and spiritually discern if it's God's will for them to marry each other.

NAOMI & CALEB

Naomi, being young and naive, fell in love with Caleb. She loved him and they dated for quite a while. Caleb got an opportunity to travel outside the country to work. During his last visit to Naomi, he asked her to wait for him. He asked her to take a blood covenant, promising she would not date anyone till he returns. Caleb held a razor blade and cut his right thumb. Naomi loved Caleb so much and thought she was never going to be able to live without him; she also didn't want to put herself in bondage. Luckily, she didn't succumb. The plan was for her to also cut her thumb and join it to his to seal the promise. What if one of them had HIV? What if one of them dies? Naomi, fortunately for her had listened during church service of how dangerous blood covenant are. Had it been that she went ahead to take the oath, they may have had to engage in several deliverance programs to be free from the bondage. Caleb travelled and never contacted Naomi again.

Amos 3:3 (MSG)

"Do two people walk hand in hand if they aren't going to the same place?"

You can't hold on to a relationship if the other party has no interest. If you really want something, pray to God about it and He'll direct you; keep praying and focus on being better. Hold on to one healthy and godly relationship. Avoid serial relationships at all cost. Do not sacrifice your purity just to keep a relationship which isn't meant to be. You can't use sex to keep a man or a woman.

Dr. D.K. Olukoya always says that "True love doesn't break the divine rule. Whatever breaks divine rules, will eventually ruin". Although God could step in and intervene, it is better not take the grace of God in vain.

As a lady, the most important factor to consider in your significant other is His love for God and the things of God. Don't be fixated on the tall, dark, rich husband mentality. You have the power to make your husband wealthy by the virtues you possess. When you look out for just the physical appearance, you get carried away and ignore the spiritual aspects of a man and how a godly foundation is a prerequisite for a sustainable home.

Proverbs 31:30 (GNT)
"Charm is deceptive and beauty disappears, but a woman who honors the LORD should be praised."

For a man, love is beyond the outer appearance of a woman. Marriage is deep and physical beauty alone won't build the home. You need a woman with a strong character; one who is willing to learn. As a man, you must be emotionally intelligent and have a strong financial plan before considering the idea of marriage. Marriage is a lifetime institution and it's worth preparing adequately for. The process should entail more prayers and counselling for things to be better for you and for your partner. There'll always be challenges but God will give you the grace to overcome.

As a lady, when you demand money from the opposite sex, you tend to be indebted and might succumb to sexual advances. That is why as a lady, you should be independent. Don't rely on the opposite sex for survival. Also, be contented with what you have. Despite the disappointment of past suitors, don't give up on God. Those who left are most times not God's intention for you. If they were meant for you, they would have stayed. You do not need to validate yourself by those who chose to leave. A broken relationship is much better than a broken marriage. Love is not blind; do not stay in a toxic relationship where your partner derives joy in beating you or in verbal assault. Seek help, pray and importantly, exit the relationship.

While in a relationship, don't share your partner's imperfections to a third party, especially the opposite sex because most times, they might capitalize on that weakness and discourage you from pursuing the relationship or act like the good person just to take advantage of the situation.

SHARON & DAVID

Sharon and David had been dating for over 3 years. David got busy with work so he can earn more and save towards their wedding and because of that he hardly had time to call Sharon as often as he used to. Sharon complained several times and had to also speak to David's best friend, Jonathan. Sharon and Jonathan got close and she kept telling him how David wronged her. Jonathan took advantage of the situation and kept giving Sharon the attention she sought for and more.

After a while, they started having an affair. Jonathan later stopped all forms of communication with Sharon when he got tired of the affair. David somehow found out about them and was extremely disappointed. He called off the relationship with Sharon and moved on with his life. David learnt not to be too busy, to the extent of ignoring his loved one. Going forward, despite his busy schedule, he made out time for his loved ones.

The attitude you'll exhibit in marriage will be a result of what you learn while single and the little things you take pleasure doing. Don't wait till you're married before you develop yourself and do the right things. Be who you want your spouse to be.

Decision Exercise:

....

....

CHAPTER 5

GROW IN YOUR RELATIONSHIP

The institution of marriage is an amazing gift from God. Finding your divine partner has nothing to do with looks, age or income. The prerequisite for a successful marriage is spiritual insight. Marriage is a lifetime institution and it is very important and powerful, so before taking such an important decision as regards marriage, you need to pray to avoid making a wrong choice. The institution of marriage plays a significant role in the destiny of a man and his family.

Marriage is to bring honour and glory to God, to the couple and it's a gift to humanity. In marriage, the goal is to fulfill your purpose together, help each other grow spiritually and make heaven eventually. You must put God at the center of your home. Any decision you make as a family must not be contrary to the will of God.

Ephesians 5:31 (GNT)
"As the scripture says, "For this reason, a man
will leave his father and mother
and unite with his wife, and the two will become one."

After a wedding, comes marriage and its sustainability is largely dependent on the grace of God and the resolve of the couple. Both parties must make conscious efforts to keep the marriage and raise godly children. There's no perfect union, perfect marriage, perfect husband, wife or perfect child. Just love each other and ensure you both make conscious effort to be happy. A family would be able to achieve more if parents plan their lives together and if they put God first in all they do. Marriage is challenging enough. Without God, it is more challenging.

Couples who celebrate 50 years marriage anniversary definitely had lot of challenges but together in unity and by the grace of God overcame there challenges. God hates divorce and the only way to avoid it is for you to marry the right person God intended for you. The devil delights in a broken home and couples should never give the enemy an opportunity to penetrate their homes. Unforgiveness is very dangerous. Forgive your spouse even before they offend you. Differences must be resolved in God's way. Invest in your marriage. Pay attention to details, discuss issues and set feasible goals together. Always try to reach a consensus and understand each other's views and perspectives. Do not record past mistakes and do not keep secrets from each other. Make your spouse your best friend. Communicate effectively and have memorable moments with your spouse.

Try as much as possible to avoid keeping late nights, knowing your spouse will be expecting you to be at home at a certain time. When caught up with work, call to inform your spouse, to avoid unnecessary panic. Marriage is for companionship, affection, the satisfaction of sexual needs and both parties should realize that marriage is a sacred obligation and faithfulness to each other and to God is a requirement for a successful marriage. Husband and wife are to be united physically, mentally, emotionally and spiritually. The husband and wife are no longer two but one in Christ. Marriage is much more beyond sex, changing one's name or raising children. We need grace for marital bliss.

Stingy husbands won't get the best from their wives and a nagging wife chases her husband away. A man must always take care of his wife because if anything goes wrong with his finances, his wife would be the one to feed him and take care of the home. Also in situations where the spouse is not financially stable, the little things you do, can go a long way and would be appreciated a lot. Little gifts, the right words and time spent with your partner can foster love and increase joy. Joy most times can be derived from little things. The stinginess of a man towards his wife and the home makes room for unnecessary arguments, which most times might lead to unhealthy fights. Financial challenges can bring tension; nevertheless, a woman must never leave her spouse because of financial imbalance. Save for the raining day, support your spouse and pray fervently.

Ephesians 5:21 (GNT)
"Submit yourselves to one another because
of your reverence for Christ"

Love God, love yourself and love your significant other. A man who does not love God would find it very difficult to love his wife, same with the woman.

1 Corinthians 7:2-6 (MSG)
" It's good for a man to have a wife, and for a woman to have a husband. Sexual drives are strong, but marriage is strong enough to contain them and provide for a balanced and fulfilling sexual life in a world of sexual disorder. The marriage bed must be a place of mutuality—the husband seeking to satisfy his wife, the wife seeking to satisfy her husband. Marriage is not a place to "stand up for your rights." Marriage is a decision to serve the other, whether in bed or out. Abstaining from sex is permissible for a period of time if you both agree to it, and if it's for the purposes of prayer and fasting— but only for such times. Then come back together again. Satan has an ingenious way of tempting us when we least expect it."

Sex within marriage is meant to help you understand God's love for you. Withholding sex and pleasurable moments is unhealthy in a marriage. Marriage is a lifetime union and it takes both parties to make the best of the marriage.

Hebrew 13:4 (MSG)
"Honour marriage and guard the sacredness of

sexual intimacy between wife and husband. God draws a firm line against casual and illicit sex".

Adultery is self-destructive and can destroy a life and marriage. On no given circumstance should you cheat on your spouse and do not give your spouse a reason to commit adultery. When a married person cheats, it steals his peace of mind and causes guilt. Marriages are different and don't compare your home, rather work with God's standard and regulations for marriage. Marriage should be enjoyed and not endured.

Marriage is a major determinant in the fulfillment of destiny. So, do not be in a hurry. Allow God to choose for you. Acquire the right information, knowledge and understanding prior to marriage. Pray for wisdom and learn to hear from God before going into marriage. Do your best to build a strong family unit. Live the word of God because what you leave in your children goes a long way in their lives, especially when you are no more.

Decision Exercise:

....

....

....

....

....

CHAPTER 6

A DESTINY WIFE

A destiny wife is a helper to her husband and also a support system to her home. A woman's worth is measured by her soul, character and values. The world needs good women who in turn would be good wives and raise godly children. She must be passionate about the things of God, does not neglect her role in her prayer closet in her home and in the society at large.

A woman of worth does not allow her gender limit her from being the best she can be, she is a great wife, mother and a very influential woman in her society and the world. A worthy woman understands the power of being educated and attaining greater heights.

A wife of inestimable value never nags. She is always there in good and bad times for her husband; even when he doesn't compliment her efforts. He notices her actions, in-actions and everything she does for him and the home. She doesn't wait for her husband to provide all her basic needs.

Ephesians 5:22-24 (GNT)
"Wives, submit yourselves to your husbands as to the Lord. For a husband has authority over his wife just as Christ has authority over the church;
and Christ is himself the Savior of the church, his body. And so wives must submit themselves completely to their husbands just as the church submits itself to Christ."

A good wife loves God, respects her husband, teaches her children good morals and can never allow her home suffer as a result of her career. A wife is a pillar of the family, to hold the family together in good and bad times. A virtuous woman never compares her husband to other men. A woman of worth, stays true to whom she really is and loves her husband unconditionally.

It is of utmost value for a woman to be creative in the kitchen, just as much as she ought to be creative in her matrimonial bed. She cooks good meals, cleans the home daily and ensures her home is a citadel of peace, joy and tranquility. She tries as much as possible to get feedback from her husband and improves in all aspect, she submits to him and supports him in all his endeavors. She prays for him and she never stops loving him.

Sirach 26:1-4 (GNT)

"The husband of a good wife is a fortunate man; he will live twice as long because of her. A fine wife is a joy to her husband, and he can live out his years in peace. A good wife is among the precious blessings given to those who fear the Lord. Whether such men are rich or poor, they will be happy and always look cheerful".

A destiny wife is an asset to her husband. She wakes up early, prays, cleans the house and gives the family healthy fruits and is conscious about their health, lifestyle and career choices.

1 Peter 3:1-6 (GNT)

"In the same way you wives must submit yourselves to your husbands so that if any of them do not believe God's word, your conduct will win them over to believe. It will not be necessary for you to say a word because they will see how pure and reverent your conduct is. You should not use outward aids to make yourselves beautiful, such as the way you fix your hair, or the jewelry you put on, or the dresses you wear. Instead, your beauty should consist of your true inner self, the ageless beauty of a gentle and quiet spirit, which is of the greatest value in God's sight. For the devout women of the past who placed their hope in God used to make themselves beautiful by submitting themselves to their husbands.

> *Sarah was like that; she obeyed Abraham and
> called him her master. You are now
> her daughters if you do good and are
> not afraid of anything."*

A woman's worth is defined by her passion for God. Her soul is as beautiful as her outward appearance. Inasmuch as she keeps her physical appearance appealing, she is also spiritually strong and grounded with the word of God.

> *Proverbs 12:4 (KJV)*
> *"A virtuous woman is a crown to her husband:
> but she that maketh
> ashamed is as rottenness in his bones"*

No man loves a nagging wife. When a man returns from work, he hopes to see a neatly arranged house, water to have his bath and good food to eat. The outside world is a bit hard and a man would be grateful to always come home, knowing his wife will welcome him and give him rest of mind after a tough day. Also, during times of misunderstanding, a destiny wife does not raise her voice or speaks rudely to her husband. She can never humiliate, disrespect or disregard her husband.

> *1 Thessalonians 4:3-5 (MSG)*
> *"Keep yourself from sexual promiscuity, learn to appreciate
> and give dignity to your body, not abusing it, as is so
> common among those who know nothing of God."*

There is an adage I came across recently, that says, ***"A woman who commits adultery is bringing a curse upon herself."***

When a woman has been joined in holy matrimony with her husband, on no circumstances should she defile her marital vows. A destiny wife stays faithful and can never commit adultery, not for pleasure or financial benefit. Every sin in secret hurts eventually. A woman should not assume her spouse is having extramarital affairs and make it a yardstick for doing the same thing. A woman, who cheats, would depreciate in value and loose her dignity.

A destiny wife plans and makes conscious efforts to invest in herself, her husband and her children. She takes life-changing decisions alongside her husband and prays to God to sustain the home. She has a homely nature and takes care of visitors and family when they visit her home. She doesn't assume her in-laws are witches. She knew her husband had a family that meant everything to him before she got married to him. She should treat his family the way she wants him to treat hers.

A woman of worth does not affiliate with worldly women who would always advise her wrongly against her husband or his family. A destiny wife does not discuss her family issues with random friends who cannot help her. A virtuous woman understands that no man is perfect and would learn to live with the imperfections of her husband. Love diminishes when you focus on the negatives; focus on the positives and help your husband become who God has called him to be.

Decision Exercise:

....
....
....
....

CHAPTER 7

A GREAT HUSBAND

It is imperative for a man to be responsible and lead by example. A great husband provides for the family. A man of purpose ought to work hard for himself, his home, and the lives he has to impact. A man cannot afford to be complacent or irresponsible. So many lives are waiting for you to succeed so you can help their destinies. A great man does not give himself to prostitutes; if he does, he may lose everything he owns. A great husband does not let his mind dwell on the beauty of any woman who is not his wife.

1 Peter 3:7 (GNT)
"In the same way, you husbands must live with your wives with the proper understanding that they are more delicate than you. Treat them with respect, because they also will receive, together with you, God's gift of life. Do this so that nothing will interfere with your prayers"

Husbands have a significant role to play in the life of their wives and family. Women are very delicate and emotional. A man needs to give his love, time and must be kind to his wife. The word of God admonishes men to love the woman they married at their youth. When a woman is cherished, she would be at peace and that would encourage her to pray for her husband. A wife's prayer for her husband is very potent.

Colossians 3:19 (MSG)
"Husbands, go all out in love for your wives.

Don't take advantage of them"

A great husband supports his wife in her quest to be all she can possibly be as a mother and a woman of substance. He prays for her, provides for her and loves her unconditionally: he supports her spiritually, financially, morally and in all aspects of her life.

Ephesians 5:25-33 (GNT)
"Men ought to love their wives just as they love their
own bodies. A man who loves his wife loves himself.
None of us ever hate our own bodies. Instead, we
feed them, and take care of them, just as Christ
does the church; for we are members of his body.)
As the scripture says, "For this reason, a man will
leave his father and mother and unite with his
wife, and the two will become one." There is a deep
secret truth revealed in this scripture, which I
understand as applying to Christ and the church. But it
also applies to you: every husband must love his wife as
himself, and every wife must respect her husband"

An uncommon husband would love and take proper care of his wife as much as he would care for himself. In marriage, you don't need to be told before you do extraordinary things for your spouse. Surprise him/her with gifts and remember to celebrate special days with each other. It will cost you a little to help your partner out with chores and running the home.

Ephesians 5:25 (GNT)
"Husbands, love your wives just as Christ
loved the church and gave his life for it"

Protect your wife and make her happy. Do not expose your wife to danger. Support her with all you have. Love is far beyond words, love is actionable. Love is revealed by what you do. Your actions should always depict love and utmost respect. Even when no man is watching, be faithful to your wife. Be happy and grateful to God for the gift of marriage. Be content with all your wife is and have. Do not give your love to some other woman.

God in heaven sees all that a man does. Careless living and an undisciplined life can end up in death.

Decision Exercise:

....
....
....
....

CHAPTER 8

Marriage, A Commitment

A marriage ordained by God can never result in divorce. Your marriage must work and your marriage will work. When something good gets broken, you fix it; you don't just throw it away. Go for proper counselling; apologize to your spouse, have a conversation, table out the issues and give love another chance; especially if there are children involved. Marriage is to honour God, husband and wife, the institution of marriage, to be a source of inspiration to the next generation, to live an exemplary life for your children and humanity.

Mark 10:6-9 (GNT)
"But in the beginning, at the time of creation, 'God made them male and female,' as the scripture says. 'And for this reason, a man will leave his father and mother and unite with his wife, and the two will become one.' So they are no longer two, but one. No human being then must separate what God has joined together."

When your spouse offends you, let go and let God. Forgive your spouse, learn from the experience and be willing to ask for forgiveness. If your spouse feels you were the one at fault, even if you were the one hurt, apologize and let peace reign.

JENNIFER & JONATHAN
Jennifer and Jonathan have been married for about two years. One certain time, she had an official assignment in another state

in the country. She travelled and informed her husband when she was scheduled to return home. She was able to finish her task at the office earlier than planned, so she decided to surprise her husband; knowing it's a weekend and he'll be at home. She got home to meet the surprise of her life; her husband was with her best friend Jessica on her matrimonial bed. She caught them having sex and was in awe of what she saw. She almost burst into anger, she also thought to herself,

> ***"Be calm. Don't fight. Avoid committing a crime that might cost you more".***

She closed the door and stepped out of the house. She cried and was pained. She trusted her husband and Jessica. Jessica was her best friend who she confided in all the time. Apparently, Jessica always admired Jonathan, even while he got married to her best friend.

Jonathan and Jessica were shocked at the way she responded. Her silence made them sober. Jonathan realized he hurt his wife so much and immediately told Jessica to leave his home and never return. They both reached out to Jennifer separately and sincerely asked for forgiveness.

Moving forward, Jennifer forgave her husband and her friend. Jennifer had a conversation with her husband and they discussed about why he cheated; the things he didn't like and what he wanted Jennifer to improve on to make their marriage better.

In life, it pays more to respond to situations than to react. Try having a healthy conversation with your loved ones and express your concerns in a subtle way. Do not reveal everything about your home to a third party.

It's best to resolve issues of infidelity God's way. A dialogue most times is a very effective remedy to resolve marital issues. Relationships, as well as marriage, deteriorate when misunderstandings are constantly ignored and not resolved. It's not just about consistent apologies, you need to be remorseful and try as much as possible to stop actions that make your significant other upset. Take it to God in prayer, as this will enable you overcome whatever struggles you have gracefully.

Matthew 5: 32 (MSG)
"If you divorce your wife, you're responsible for making her an adulteress (unless she has already made herself that by sexual promiscuity). And if you marry such a divorced adulteress, you're automatically an adulterer yourself. You can't use legal cover to mask a moral failure".

A broken home, if not properly managed, can lead to juvenile delinquency in children. In situations of domestic violence in marriage, seek help, go for professional counselling, talk to the dearest person to your spouse and allow God fix it. Do not keep quiet in an abusive or violent marriage and hope things would get better; despite all the positive attempts to stop the abusive acts of your partner.

Understand your partner and that pray God would touch their heart. Most times our reaction to situations are what triggers violence. Seek for wisdom from above to know what to do in every circumstance. For instance, if you suspect or caught your spouse cheating, instead of taking drastic measures such as raining insulting words or fighting, walk away. Keep praying for your spouse to have a change of heart, so as to acknowledge that marriage is sacred and the marital bed is undefiled. How you positively reacted to the
situation would make him or her appreciate God in your life. It may even make them fear God and love you more; never to hurt you ever again.

Be very prayerful and protect your family, marriage and spouse. No weapon formed against your family shall prosper. Beware of dangerous distractions that destroy homes made in heaven.

Weaknesses such as lack of forgiveness, greed, self-centeredness, hatred, disgust, and strife towards one's partner can contribute to the tension in the home. As a couple, work on your attitude; avoid unnecessary arguments or hatred that would lead to one partner considering divorce. Divorce exposes the other partner to all forms of sexual sins and it destroys the soul even more. Live up to your marital vows. God hates divorce.

For a sustainable home, you need to forgive quickly. Do not compare your spouse to another, pray daily, respect each other, avoid third-party involvement as much as possible, appear appealing to your spouse, laugh a lot and share everything with each other. Marriage is a lifetime commitment; do not let evil come into your home. Avoid anger, hot-temper, un-forgiveness, verbal and physical violence, stinginess, carelessness, negative advice and greed. Pray and let God fight for you. It's going to be worth the fight. Your marriage is worth fighting for, if you want it to work. A peaceful home is a crucial aspect of fulfilling your divine assignment.

The institution of marriage is very powerful. It's a formidable union of a man and woman: two human beings becoming one. The devil doesn't like the union of marriage and would do anything to make things go sour. Pray, ask God to help you. God can restore your marriage. Fight for your marriage in prayer. Don't ever give up.

Decision Exercise:

....

....

....

CHAPTER 9

Nurture Relationships

Family is everything. Our relationship with our family has a tremendous impact in our lives. Your family most times would be ready to protect you even when others desert you. Our attitude towards our loved ones, most times, reflects in the way they treat us.

Deuteronomy 5: 16 (MSG)
"Respect your father and mother—GOD, your God, commands it! You'll have a long life; the land that God is giving you will treat you well"

Your attitude towards your parents matters a whole lot in life. Respect and obey them. Do not compare your parents with others. Be content with all they have to offer you.

Proverbs 20:20 (MSG)
"Anyone who curses his father and mother extinguishes light and exists benighted"

Do not use insulting words on your parents. The actions of your parents should not be misinterpreted. Whatever they may do, they most times, mean well for you. Sometimes, parents are strict towards their children because they love them and want the best for them. Whenever you offend your parent(s) or an elderly person, apologize sincerely till you are forgiven. The first commandment is for young people to respect their parents and the reward is that all may go well with them and they may live long.

Proverbs 23:22-25 (MSG)
"Listen with respect to the father who raised you, and when your mother grows old, don't neglect her. Buy truth—don't sell it for love or money; buy wisdom, buy education, buy insight. Parents rejoice when their children turn out well; wise children become proud parents. So make your father happy! Make your mother proud!"

Always respect your parents' foresight and judgments. Don't be carried away by how some people neglect their parents. A child who always makes her/ his parents happy would constantly be showered with prayers and those prayers, most times, manifest.

Proverbs 19:26 (GNT)
"Only a shameful, disgraceful person wo uld mistreat his father or turn his mother away from his home"

A troublesome and disrespectful child steals the peace of mind from her/ his parents, which, most times, result in depression and other health related issues.

Your Life, Your Legacy

Most times, people do what they see you do. They imitate your actions. So note that you have a vital role to play in others people's lives. You have to be conscious of your own attitude and actions. Your life is a mirror and the world is watching you. Your character affects nearly everything else. Go all out to make the lives of others better. Show unconditional love, compassion to the lives around you.

Show love to your parents, siblings, relatives, friends and acquaintances. That's the only way they would be willing to do more and help you fulfill your purpose. No man is indispensable. You can't do it all by yourself. You need the grace of God and human resources to actualize your purpose. Help your friends in difficult times, when you can; encourage and inspire them. Take a conscious effort to be dependable and reliable.

1 Timothy 5:8 (GNT)
"But if any do not take care of their relatives,
especially the members of their
own family, they have denied the faith and
are worse than an unbeliever."

Create a healthy work-life balance: make time for family. Do not let your home suffer as a result of your job. God has entrusted your family to you and you need to protect their wellbeing the best way you can. Communicate often with your parents, your significant other, siblings and relatives. Your nuclear family is very important. Build a very strong family unit and set priorities. In life, you can't please everyone.

What type of friend or family member are you? Your actions and inactions can directly or indirectly affect people. You need to take that conscious effort to love everyone around you even if what you receive in return is hatred. Love, without judgment. You need to be a good and reliable friend to attract good and reliable friends.

Our peers always seem to have some influence over us. Be careful of the kind of friends you keep. Life is too short to dwell on things and people who make you unhappy. If you have a friend who keeps hurting you, forgive the person, have a dialogue as regards your concerns and move on. Surround yourself with good people and be intentional about the people you call your friends. A friend should be able to lift you up positively and spiritually and not someone who would intentionally pulls you down or torment you.

Honour your leaders, love them. Encourage your fellow man, reach out and help whenever you can. Avoid offending other people. Look out for the best in others. Surround yourself with like-minded, positive people who want to succeed. Ensure you pay attention to your self-image, relationship with others and attitude to people. If you notice you have a set of friends or a friend who is leading you down the wrong path, try as much as possible to cut away from that friendship before it leads you into trouble.

1 JOHN 2:9-11 (MSG)
"Anyone who claims to live in God's light and hates a brother or sister is still in the dark. It's the person who loves brother and sister who dwells in God's light and doesn't block the light from others. But whoever hates is still in the dark, stumbles around in the dark, doesn't know which end is up, blinded by the darkness"

Love one another, care for each other and be conscious of your actions towards your fellow man. Hatred in the heart of a man brings nothing but destruction and unhappiness. Forgive those who have intentionally hurt you. Watch and pray, follow the instructions of God and associate with the wise. There are friends you must take conscious efforts to keep and some you must never keep. Understand the seasons of people in your life and enjoy the journey.

Matthew 5:44 (GNT)
"love your enemies and pray for those who persecute you"

Demonstrate God's love towards people even when they are unfair towards you. Be quick to forgive and bless them.

Matthew 7:1-5 (GNT)
"Do not judge others, so that God will not judge you, for God will judge you in the same way as you judge others, and he

will apply to you the same rules you apply to others. Why, then, do you look at the speck in your brother's eye, and pay no attention to the log in your own eye? How dare you say to your brother, 'Please, let me take that speck out of your eye,' when you have a log in your own eye? You hypocrite! First, take the log out of your own eye, and then you will be able to see clearly to take the speck out of your brother's eye."

Do not judge anyone. No one has a perfect life. Rather than analyzing someone's imperfections, focus on your journey. Simply mind your business. Time spent judging others should be reinvested in self-development.

Matthew 7:6 (GNT)
"Do not give what is holy to dogs — they will only turn and attack you. Do not throw your pearls in front of pigs — they will only trample them underfoot."

In life, trust but do not have absolute trust. Be careful who you entrust things to. Pray at all times, for a discerning spirit.

Decision Exercise:

....
....
....
....

CHAPTER 10

Habits

The devil is the prince of this world and he has the power to make evil and destructive habits seem easy and without consequences. The devil can manipulate a man such that he might not be aware that he's being manipulated; he will wallow in sin and self-destructive acts until it eventually kills him.

1 John 3:8-9 (KJV)
"He that committed sin is of the devil; for the devil sinneth from the beginning. For this purpose, the Son of God was manifested, that he might destroy the works of the devil. Whosoever is born of God doth not commit sin; for his seed remaineth in him: and he cannot sin, because he is born of God."

God is so merciful; He gives everyone the ability to make a choice and gives them several opportunities to repent. He has given us a conscience to discern what is right from wrong. An individual can choose to be filled with the Holy Spirit or be filled with the devil. The Holy Spirit gives life but the devil came solely to steal, kill and destroy.

1 Timothy 2:22 (GNT)
"Avoid the passions of youth, and strive for righteousness, faith, love, and peace, together with those who with a pure heart call out to the Lord for help."

Some vices are peculiar to the youthful season. Destructive habits have the tendency to get young people trapped and can mar their future. Destructive lifestyles could disrupt the God-ordained journey of an individual. It could make the attainment of goals last longer than God's actual plan. Fleeing youthful lust to an extent would help spare a lot of sad regrets, sorrows, pain and sad memories.

Passions of youth are seen in the predominant aspect of drugs and sexuality. Substance abuse can be addictive and dangerous to human health. It's a temporary relief to a problem but in the long run it causes more harm to an individual than good.

DANIEL

Daniel was born into a low-income class home. His parents were petty traders and they struggled to take care of the home front. He had eight siblings and as the first child, he was expected to figure out how to take care of his younger ones. Daniel dropped out from school because his parent could not afford the fees and his upkeep. He hawked and sold
all kind of things, just to make ends meet. Daniel grew up in a harsh environment. He started mixing with friends who introduced him to selling hard drugs and over time he got addicted to taking them himself. He sometimes took these harmful substances in order to seek solace and forget his troubles. Soon after the effect of the drugs cleared, he gets drowned in depression again. Daniel's addiction got worse and at a point he left his home and started living in the streets. Daniel's addiction affected him badly and caused him to be mentally unstable.

Substance intake are temporary relieve to problems that may remain if nothing constructive is done about them. It has a drastic and deadly repercussion on users. Many have lost their precious lives as a result of excessive intake of alcohol. Excessive intake of alcohol leads to drunkenness and when drunk, individuals loses consciousness of themselves and acts in an unusual way.

COSMOS

Cosmos was a very handsome young man. He was also very brilliant and had the highest Cumulative Grade Points Average (C.G.P.A) while in the University. Every girl on campus wanted to have him. One night, he decided to go clubbing with his friends. He didn't take alcohol but he had a bottle of soft drink as he enjoyed the music. While activities were going on, he felt pressed and needed to use the rest room. He trusted his friends to look after his drink. On his return, all his friends had gone to the dance floor. He was reluctant taking his drink but reconsidered and finished it.

A few minutes later, he felt uneasy and approached one of his friends who advised him to head back to the hostel and rest. His friends were still having fun, so he left alone. A few minutes after he left, he started vomiting blood and was rushed to the hospital by some Good Samaritan. Unfortunately, he didn't make it to the hospital before he gave up the ghost. Autopsy later revealed he was poisoned.

Proverbs 20:1 (MSG)
"Wine makes you mean, beer makes you
quarrelsome— a staggering
drunk is not much fun"

HARRISON

Harrison is known to always drink and get drunk. Whenever he was drunk, he said everything about his life and family to those around him. He reveals both good and bad secrets of his life, his plans and aspirations. The world is wicked and not everyone is happy to see his fellow man progress.

Drunkenness gives the wicked an avenue to penetrate and harm a man. A drunken fellow is most times mocked by those around him. If one is drunk and decides to drive, the individual could run into vehicles, a ditch and this could destroy lives and properties and even lead to death. Those moments during a hangover, the individual is a total waste and can never do anything fruitful till the alcohol fades. Drunkenness is a profitless and useless venture.

Proverbs 23:29-30 (GNT)
"Show me people who drink too much, who have to try out fancy drinks, and I will show you, people, who are miserable and sorry for themselves, always causing trouble and always complaining. Their eyes are bloodshot, and they have bruises that could have been avoided. Don't let wine tempt you, even though it is rich red, and it sparkles in the cup, and it goes down smoothly. The next morning you will feel as if you had been bitten by a poisonous snake. Weird sights will appear before your eyes, and you will not be able to think or speak clearly. You will feel as if you were out on the ocean, seasick, swinging high up in the rigging of a tossing ship. "I must have been hit," you will say; "I must have been beaten up, but I don't remember it. Why can't I wake up? I need another drink."

Opportunities can be missed when a person gets drunk and wasted. A man's masculinity cannot be validated by his ability to drink and get drunk. Women who drink and get drunk can become vulnerable to sexual abuse by those who gave them the drink. Don't leave your life to chance.

Ephesians 5:18-20 (MSG)
"Don't drink too much wine. That cheapens your life. Drink the Spirit of God, huge draughts of him. Sing hymns instead of drinking songs! Sing songs from your heart to Christ. Sing praises over everything, any excuse for a song to God the Father in the name of our Master, Jesus Christ."

Say No to Smoking
Asides alcohol intake, smoking is another harmful substance to the body. It makes the consumer liable to die young; it can

lead to cancer, heart disease and shortens the victims' lifespan. Substances in cigarettes are addictive. Users ascertain they are lured into substance abuse by peers or the environment they find themselves. No reason can justify negative habits which are useless and cause more harm than good. It's one of the leading causes of death, increases the risk of cardiovascular diseases, damages the respiratory system and can also cause infertility.

Claims that smoking ameliorates minor depression are totally false. The harm it causes much later is detrimental to an individual's wellbeing and it has a devastating effect. The need to escape the reality of situations make one a drug addict not the drug itself. However, the problem still persists.

Many are aware of the dangers of smoking, yet get so involved anyway. Cigarette manufacturers and dealers are in business to the detriment of the customer who abuses the product. To quit requires the grace of God and determination when one is addicted. Identify the moments that trigger smoking, have replacements and avoid gatherings where people smoke and if possible, get help.

Abstinence

Another very critical destructive lifestyle is pre-marital sex. The carelessness at which people have sex is an indication of the value they place on themselves. When the mind of a youth is idle and unproductive, wondering thought like sex will come in and take control. Watch and pray, to avoid falling into temptation. For an individual to be able to resist sexual temptation successfully, he has to surrender totally to God. Women should test a man's declaration of love and wait until they are married before giving in to him sexually.

If an individual engages in premarital sex, it's either she/ he becomes addicted to it or she/ he detests it. It is best to patiently wait till marriage. Sex is not synonymous to love. Love is unconditional and you do not need to prove your sincere love for your partner by having sex. Sex before marriage is a sin before God and against your body. Premarital sex, extramarital affairs and all other sexual habits destroy one's relationship with God. Sex before marriage can sometimes get in the way and cause people to stay together who probably should be apart.

Sex starts from the mind and it's dangerous to lust after someone you are not married to. Think about the chances of a leaky condom or being caught in the spur of the moment and having sex without protection. Just that one time without a condom might result in unplanned parenthood, pregnancy or a truncated destiny for an individual.

A significant percentage of unplanned pregnancies lead young people into taking drastic choices, including abortion. Abortion is the conscious termination of a human life or the natural expulsion of a fetus from the womb before it is able to survive independently. The emotional trauma or physical discomfort, public humiliation, fear of not being able to cater for a child, fear of people's opinion, shame, rape cases, continuous intake of contraceptives are some of the unjustified reasons why people commit abortion. It's still not justifiable. Abortion done without a health reason is a sin. Abortion has an adverse effect on the overall health of a woman and endangers lives.

A significant percentage of ladies who undergo abortion at abortion clinics never survive. Some abortion drugs can cause liver, kidney damage, cancer and infections due to punctures. These could lead to problems in the future, such as the inability to conceive, ruptured womb, miscarriages, premature birth and sometimes death. Abortion is synonymous with murder; a lady's womb could be destroyed as a result of multiple abortions or as a result of a careless abortion procedure. A person would be called to account for killing an unborn child. So, in God's eyes, killing an unborn child is murder. Do not ever abort a child or advise a person to abort and as a doctor, do not specialize in abortion.

Having a child outside of wedlock is not the end of the world.

God is interested in you and there are graces in mistakes. Despite being put in a family way, having a child is much better than committing abortion. Be encouraged and be strong, pray for God to reveal himself to you and direct your path. The world might tag the child a bastard but that's not what God has written about the child. Own up to the mistakes made, take up the responsibility to take care of the child and prevent the child from repeating the same mistake you made. God would give you the grace to survive. Despite past mistakes, our Heavenly Father would never forsake you. Teach and train the child in the way of the Lord.

Acknowledge that the sin was fornication and avoid it at all cost. Sex outside marriage makes one feel guilty, broken, and vulnerable to sexually transmitted diseases and sometimes unplanned parenthood. Some men might not want to marry a lady who has children as a result of a careless past (who will blame them for not wanting to deal with excesses?) So be wise. God will perfect all that concerns you.

1 Thessalonians 4:4-5 (MSG)
"Learn to appreciate and give dignity to your
body, not abusing it, as is so common among
those who know nothing of God."

Sex is good and is of God but it's been thoroughly abused by mankind. The testosterone of the natural man is strong but it needs to be put under control. Sex is designed to promote God's divine purpose for man and to unite a man and his wife. A relationship built on sexual pleasure is a relationship built on lust and it may not be sustainable.

Right now, nobody is interested in the things you do in secret because you are yet to fulfill purpose. When an individual begins to fulfill purpose and begins to come into the limelight, the world would take their time to dig out the person's secrets just to pull the individual down. So why engage in activities that would be disastrous eventually. If there is no other reason to embrace purity, do it because of your destiny; it is greater than your present. Your destiny is bigger than you.

Great and powerful men have been brought down to their knees by the power of sex. The sex urge is the strongest urge in human nature. It has built and destroyed men and women. Sex also helps transmit diseases such as HIV/AIDS and other sexually transmitted diseases. A person who has no control over his/ her sexual urge should not expect to be protected against mishaps.

So many young people have been lured into believing dangerous lies and myths. There are blatant misconceptions among millennials such as it's not cool to be celibate, everyone is having sex so should, a man cannot love you except you first have sex with him, having sex just once won't get you pregnant, you need to test your partner first to be sure you are sexually compatible. The more sexual partners you have, the more of a man or woman you become. These are all blatant lies. These misconceptions lead young people nowhere. Embrace purity; embrace God. It's cool to be celibate, even if everyone around you is having premarital sex; the fear of God in you would make your choices different.

A man or woman who is God ordained for you would not leave you because you refused to have sex while in a relationship. If they're meant for you, they wouldn't leave you.

Morality is compromised when young people engage in premarital sex. We live in a sexually permissive society. Graphic displays of sexuality can be seen on television and social media. Our socialization process inculcates inappropriate values in the subconscious mind of this growing generation. Be careful what you feed your mind. Avoid feeding your mind with pornographic displays or sexual scenes for the purpose of sexual arousal; through books, magazines, online content, pictures, videos and a host of other means. These obscene materials foster rape, domestic violence, sexual dysfunction, child abuse and sexual perverseness. Pornography is unhealthy and raises unrealistic expectations of sex from your significant other or loved one.

Come to think of it, have you seen purpose driven couples in the world display sexual contents of themselves? Or a man who genuinely loves his wife, display a video of themselves during sexual activities on the internet? I don't think so. That is probably because sex is sacred and honorable. It will be disrespectful to do that to your partner. Porn stars are actors. They are in business and the scenes are for their personal gains, in order to lure consumers to pay for their content, directly or indirectly. The aftermath leaves an individual drained.

Watching pornography creates an appetite for sex and most times forces one to have negative thoughts and compromise on his values, just to satisfy the lust of the flesh. The time spent watching X-rated movies can jeopardize relationships, work performance, personal development and spiritual growth. Time spent on watching these could be reinvested into productive activities that will lead to a better life. Do not engage in activities that would drain you emotionally, physically and of course spiritually. Do not feed your mind with destructive thoughts.

Don't jeopardize your happiness and that of your loved ones. Be mindful of what you consume; it will reflect in your attitude. Pornography is artificial and not real. When an individual gets addicted to pornography, he begins to compare his/ her partner with a porn star and will expect them to perform that way. Pornography cannot satisfy emotional intimacy.

Self-sexual pleasure; a noxious habit which has the potency to affect progress and makes the individual not find pleasure in sex with his/ her partner in future. There is a tendency for a person to be dissatisfied with life with feelings of guilt, which sometimes take over and makes the individual feel dirty. With constant repetition, the brain gets wired to the action and addiction sets in. Masturbation is like every other sin. No sin is greater than another.

Naomi was addicted to self-sexual pleasure; she knew the act drained her and made her feel guilty. She prayed on several occasions and really wanted to stop the act then decided to figure out what turns her on sexually and flee them. She stopped watching pornographic movies, so as to avoid compromising her new set of moral standards. The temptation for one to give in to self-induced sex comes from what one feeds his/ her mind with. It comes from within. Eventually she stopped consuming X-rated contents and replaced the time she spent watching pornography with explicit content; reading and feeding her mind with the word of God. She also avoided idle moments when she was alone.

The sexuality of a man has a lot to do with his spirituality and how far he goes in life. Sexuality has a great influence on the world's problems. It will be wise to engage in sexual activities at the appropriate time, which is in the context of marriage. God planted the hormone in us and it takes discipline for a man not to follow the direction of his erection but subject himself to discipline and patience.

The man who is unfaithful to his wife and says "no one will ever know" is only afraid of other people but doesn't realize that God is Omniscient and sees everything we do, even when we try to hide it.

We live in a sexually confused and painful world. People have become slaves to their desires. Much of what we see, read and hear daily are fabricated in order to manipulate our emotions, attitudes and wallets. Abstinence is the ultimate protection against any form of disease or vulnerability.

Be careful of the content you put out and that which you feed your mind with daily. Do not be controlled by lust. Keep your passion in check. If an individual allows his flesh to control his every desire, he will be a joke to his enemies. The enemy would penetrate the life of a careless man easily.

Sirach 19:2-4 (GNT)
"Wine and women make sensible men do foolish things.
A man who goes to prostitutes gets more and more
careless, and that carelessness will cost him his life"

Some will say, "I am allowed to do anything". Yes, but everything is not good for you. The body is not to be used for sexual immorality but to serve God. Do you know that a man, who joins his body to a prostitute, becomes physically one with her?

1 Corinthians 6:18-20 (GNT)
"Avoid immorality. Any other sin a man commits
does not affect his body, but
the man who is guilty of sexual immorality sins against
his own body. Don't you know that your body is the
temple of the Holy Spirit, who lives in you and who was
given to you by God? You do not belong to yourselves but
to God. Avoid immorality. Any other sin a man commits
does not affect his body, but the man who is guilty of
sexual immorality sins against his own body. he bought
you for a price. So use your bodies for God's glory."

Let's ask ourselves the following questions;

- Is love equivalent to sex?
- Is it all relationships that involve sexual contact that lasts?

There are so many happenings. We need to understand God's purpose for sexuality in a positive way. Sex outside marriage sometimes results in emptiness, guilt, brokenness, fear, a feeling of being used, unloved (by God and others) and confusion. These feelings may be daunting but they disappear eventually through remorse, prayer, counselling and confession to God. God has the ability to heal and restore our dignity.

Romans 6:1-4 GNT admonishes us to be dead to sin but alive

in union with Christ. "What shall we say, then? Should we continue to live in sin so that God's grace will increase? Certainly not! We have died to sin—how then can we go on living in it? For surely you know that when we were baptized into union with Christ Jesus, we were baptized into union with his death. By our baptism, then, we were buried with him and shared his death, in order that, just as Christ was raised from death by the glorious power of the Father, so also we might live a new life."

Realize your mistakes and avoid any form of lust. We sin daily and God's love for us is amazing; He is always willing to forgive us. God wants to restore our purity. Though the physical consequences can sometimes be inevitable; the emotional and spiritual effect of sex outside of marriage is nothing compared to the former. One must refrain from any form of sexual activity outside of marriage. The grace of God is sufficient. Be steadfast, put your body under subjection, cherish your body as much as you cherish your life and most importantly, fear God.

Prayerfully deal with your weakness and anything that makes you vulnerable. Do not make yourself susceptible to the devil and his devices. As a lady, try as much as possible not to visit your male friends in their homes or in a secluded place. Do not acquiesce to an invite to visit a man or a stranger in an unknown location. Always inform your family or friends whenever you are going out.

SHARON

Sharon met a young man on her way home one certain evening. They exchanged contacts and kept communicating with each other. He was twice her age. She was excited about him, especially because he gave her cash gifts whenever she visits him. One certain day, he called and told her about an accident he had. Sharon went over to his house as usual to check up on him. He was home with his bandaged legs and was in pains. She cuddled him and cared for him. Later, he stood up from the bed, locked the door and increased the sound of the music he was playing to the highest. He removed his entire clothes and tried to force himself on her. She screamed but the music was louder than the sound of her voice. She tried to hit his injured leg but that didn't work. Sharon begged him not to deflower her but he won't let go. He kept insisting and said, "Why do you think I give you money, do you think I don't know what I am doing? Now that you are going into University, all those small boys would sleep with you and destroy your life." Sharon kept pleading but when she had no strength in her, she prayed in her mind. She prayed for God to touch his heart and grant her freedom. All of a sudden, he left her. Immediately, Sharon stood up, unlocked the door and ran away.

Prior to this incident, Sharon thought she had the strength to kick or resist being raped when found in a compromising situation. Men are strong and most times can overpower ladies and have their way. Be careful.

James 4:7 (GNT)

"So then, submit yourselves to God. Resist the Devil, and he will run away from you."

When you're with God, the devil would have no say in how you live your life. When you have passion for the things of God, the kingdom of darkness would be threatened by your existence. As a lady, avoid wearing indecent clothes, dress modestly to avoid calling for unnecessary attention.

1 Corinthians 12: 9-10 (MSG)

"My grace is enough; it's all you need. My strength comes into its own in your weakness. Once I heard that I was glad to let it happen. I quit focusing on the handicap and began appreciating the gift. It was a case of Christ's strength moving in on my weakness.

> *Now I take limitations in stride, and with good cheer,
> these limitations that cut me down to size—abuse,
> accidents, opposition, bad breaks. I just let Christ take
> over! And so the weaker I get, the stronger I become."*

A character is an extended habit and if it's a negative habit, it could become a weakness. Just as you gradually developed a habit, you can conscious efforts to eliminate it. Deal with your weaknesses and God will give you strength. Don't nurture any habit you know is detrimental to your growth. When an individual harbours a negative habit, it has the tendency to destroy their destiny if care is not taken. Every man has a weakness. Don't allow your weakness to destroy you.

Understand that mistakes are life's lessons. Mistakes are graces. All you have experienced in life is to teach you a lesson you should not to repeat it the second time. Mistakes and failures make you stronger; don't let the past rob you of your future. God has something better for you. Do not be imprisoned by your past. Learn and move on. As an individual, once you decide to forge ahead, be dead to the past life and be rest assured God is aware. Be intentional about everything and all things, good or bad, would work for your good.

1 Thessalonians 5:4-8 (MSG)
*"But friends, you're not in the dark, so how could you
be taken off guard by any of this? You're sons of Light,
daughters of Day. We live under wide open skies and know
where we stand. So let's not sleepwalk through life like those
others. Let's keep our eyes open and be smart. People sleep
at night and get drunk at night. But not us! Since we're
creatures of Day, let's act like it. Walk out into the daylight
sober, dressed up in faith, love, and the hope of salvation"*

Stay away from anything that relates to 'death' such as promiscuity, lust, greed, lies and the likes. You must decide to live a new life of love, be even-tempered, contented with all God has blessed you with, be kind, be compassionate and be quick to forgive and let go. Acknowledge and appreciate God in your journey through life. Do not put your hope in man. Many a time, we put all our hopes in our fellow human and believe they are the ones to trust for a better life, not knowing we ought to seek the face of God, and pray. God would touch the heart of your helpers and send them to you in at the right time.

Decision Exercise:

....

....

....

CHAPTER 11

Discipline, A Virtue

In life, temptations will surely come but God has already given you the grace to overcome them all.

1 Corinthians 2:5 (KJV)
"That your faith should not stand in the wisdom
of men, but in the power of
God."

What is written in the Bible cannot be changed by what is happening in the world. Despite the ills on earth, God's standard on how we should live our lives is written in the Holy Book. Holiness within and without is all that is needed to get connected to God.

Galatians 5:16-21 (GNT)
"What I say is this: let the Spirit direct your lives, and you will not satisfy the desires of the human nature. For what our human nature wants is opposed to what the Spirit wants, and what the Spirit wants is opposed to what our human nature wants. These two are enemies, and this means that you cannot do what you want to do. If the Spirit leads you, then you are not subject to the Law. What human nature does is quite plain. It shows itself in immoral, filthy, and indecent actions; in worship of idols and witchcraft. People become enemies and they fight; they become jealous, angry, and ambitious. They separate into parties and groups; they are envious, get drunk, have orgies, and do other

*things like these. I warn you now as I have before: those who
do these things will not possess the Kingdom of God"*

Imagine a person who lives well, treats others right, keeps good relationships, doesn't make man or object his gods, doesn't seduce his neighbour's spouse, doesn't indulge in casual sex, doesn't bully anyone, doesn't pile up bad debts, doesn't steal, gives to the needy, doesn't exploit the poor, is not greedy, doesn't treat one person better than another but lives by God's' statutes and faithfully honours and obeys them. This person who lives upright and well shall inherit the kingdom of God. Be a true friend of God, flee from every appearance of evil; do not tell lies or cheat people and take the work of God seriously.

Titus 2:12-13 (GNT)
*"That grace instructs us to give up ungodly living
and worldly passions, and to
live self-controlled, upright, and godly lives
in this world, as we wait for the
blessed Day we hope for, when the glory of our
great God and Savior Jesus Christ
will appear."*

An individual can party all night and not return home. Compromising gatherings, such as these, could make one susceptible to being poisoned, raped, killed, get involved in accidents, get initiated unconsciously and all sort of terrible consequences. Remember the maxim,

*"Try as much as possible to always be at the
right place at the right time."*

Never you be in a place you know the grace of God won't protect you. Don't abuse the sufficiency of God's mercies. The law (commandments) is to help us to be disciplined. God wants you to be holy and undefiled.

There are certain places that you will go to and the angels of

God assigned to guide and protect you can't go to. In such situations, if anything evil is about to befall you, you'll be left to handle it alone. We have the freedom to act but our actions, inactions, and choices either make or mar our future; Exposure has both negative and positive sides. Why do young people do things they won't want their parents to be aware of? Living a disciplined life entails a whole lot of sacrifices.

When we live God's way, we become affectionate, have deep convictions about life, become loyal, patient and have the ability to direct our energies wisely. Living a disciplined life would help you in leaving a positive legacy on earth. The best way you can live a disciplined life is to first itemize your weakness, ask God to take control, make decisions and ensure you take steps towards it daily. Living a disciplined life would make you a responsible and a better person.

Youthful exuberance can result in elongated years of struggle. A journey of four years could be extended for forty years if precautions are not taken. As a student, concentrate in school, avoid negative friends, clubbing and examination malpractice. As a worker, be sincere in your dealings; be hard working, innovative and diligent. As a single youth, be prayerful, disciplined and keep yourself. As a married person, be faithful to your spouse and appreciate them daily. Tell your husband you love him, tell your wife she's beautiful and always appreciate her. As a parent, train your child in the way of the Lord.

Young people should not be carried away by the lust of the flesh. Do not let the desire for money, fame and worldly activities get in the way of your success. People are watching you and the things you do. Do not think no one is paying attention. You need to stand for Christ and be known for that. Let your "Yes" be "Yes" and "No" be "No". Do not trade your integrity for what you think you want. Do not trade your virtue for material gains as you might end up being guilty and unhappy at the end.

A person's character to an extent determines how far he or she would go in life. Be sincere, care for others, be compassionate and respect others. Be true to yourself and focus on what is important.

2 Timothy 3:16-17 (GNT)
"All Scripture is inspired by God and is useful for
teaching the truth, rebuking error, correcting faults,
and giving instruction for right living, so that
the person who serves God may be fully qualified
and equipped to do every kind of good deed."

God has given you the power to live a better life and to make the world a better place. Through God's word, you are equipped to live holy and triumph through life.

Decision Exercise:

....

....

....

....

....

CHAPTER 12

THE STORM WILL NOT LAST

What happens when life knocks you down? Resilience makes you strong in down times and the comeback is always rewarding when you trust God. God is capable of helping you find peace in times of pain. Relax; don't be so preoccupied with getting so you can respond to God's giving. Do not complain; be hopeful, joyful and patient.

Luke 12:29-32 (MSG)
"Protect yourself against the least bit of greed.
Life is not defined by what you have, even when
you have a lot. There is far more to your inner life
than the food you put in your stomach"

There is nobody in life that does not have challenges. If you are to be sad as a result of a challenge, it means you are going to be sad for a very long time. Why not stay happy always, irrespective and be content with what God has already blessed you with? Thank God for all He has blessed you with then work hard towards what you want.

Corinthians 10:13 (MSG)
"No test or temptation that comes your way is beyond
the course of what others have had to face. All you
need to remember is that God will never let you down;
he'll never let you be pushed past your limit; he'll
always be there to help you come through it"

As you grow through the various stages of life, a new challenge will arise. How you react or respond to each of them is what is most important. There is no challenge in life that God has not made a provision for you to overcome. Pass through challenges but don't dwell on them. Focus on God and not your situation. Don't murmur or complain to people who cannot help your situation. Sadness is a waste of time and it will drain you completely of all you've got, if care isn't taken.

Failure builds your confidence; it makes you better. It's an indication that at least you have made an attempt to make something work.

James 1:12-15 (MSG)

"Anyone who meets a testing challenge head-on and manages to stick it out is mighty fortunate. For such persons loyally in love with God, the reward is life and more life. Don't let anyone under pressure to give in to evil say, "God is trying to trip me up." God is impervious to evil and puts evil in no one's way. The temptation to give in to evil comes from us and only us. We have no one to blame but the leering, seducing flare-up of our own lust. Lust gets pregnant, and has a baby: sin! Sin grows up to adulthood, and becomes a real killer."

God cannot tempt you. Temptations are from the devil and in these times, your faith is put to test and the fear of God in you would determine your actions. Nothing in life kills more than ignorance. Even though God forgives when you err and you seek forgiveness, the earthly consequence of those negative decisions arises. Always think about the end of your choice before you even make that choice.

1 Corinthians 4:7-12 (MSG)

"If you only look at us, you might well miss the brightness. We carry this precious Message around in

> *the unadorned clay pots of our ordinary lives. That's*
> *to prevent anyone from confusing God's incomparable*
> *power with us. As it is, there's not much chance of that.*
> *You know for yourselves that we're not much to look at.*
> *We've been surrounded and battered by troubles, but*
> *we're not demoralized; we're not sure what to do, but we*
> *know that God knows what to do; we've been spiritually*
> *terrorized, but God hasn't left our side; we've been thrown*
> *down, but we haven't broken. What they did to Jesus,*
> *they do to us—trial and torture, mockery and murder;*
> *what Jesus did among them, he does in us—he lives! Our*
> *lives are at constant risk for Jesus' sake, which makes*
> *Jesus' life all the more evident in us. While we're going*
> *through the worst, you're getting in on the best!"*

The spiritual controls the physical. A strong prayer life leads to spiritual empowerment to enable you surmount any challenge in life. If one doesn't use the weapon of prayer effectively, others who use negative power might overcome that person. Safeguard your heart by meditating on the word of God. Wait patiently for God and He'll meet you at the point of your need.

Job 14:14 (KJV)
"Man that is born of a woman is of
few days and full of trouble."

We live in a wicked world, where evil is pre-dominant and lives are used to replace lives, destinies are stolen and frustration sets into the life of the victim. The moment the wicked sees an individual has a potential to be great in life, he would go all out to destroy it; that is when challenges arise. To scale through life at this point, you'll need God's grace.

2 Corinthians 4:15-18 (MSG)
"Every detail works to your advantage and to God's glory:
more and more grace, more and more people, more and more

> *praise! So we're not giving up. How could we! Even though*
> *on the outside it often looks like things are falling apart*
> *on us, on the inside, where God is making new life, not a*
> *day goes by without his unfolding grace. These hard times*
> *are small potatoes compared to the coming good times, the*
> *lavish celebration prepared for us. There's far more here than*
> *meets the eye. The things we see now are here today, gone*
> *tomorrow. But the things we can't see now will last forever."*

Courage in the midst of battles is a prerequisite to overcome. It takes courage to stay calm in this world. Fear, regrets and self-condemnation deters progress. Rather than dwell on the reasons why a situation went wrong, fix it and move forward. Make sure you are not stagnant. Keep moving. Focus on God.

> *1 Peter 5:8-11 (MSG)*
> *"Keep a cool head. Stay alert. The Devil is poised to pounce*
> *and would like nothing better than to catch you napping.*
> *Keep your guard up. You're not the only ones plunged into*
> *these hard times. It's the same with Christians all over*
> *the world. So keep a firm grip on the faith. The suffering*
> *won't last forever. It won't be long before this generous*
> *God who has great plans for us in Christ— eternal and*
> *glorious plans they are!—will have you put together and*
> *on your feet for good. He gets the last word; yes, he does."*

Be gentle and don't be too hard on yourself. Believe God in his word: challenging times don't last forever. Poverty is not a disease but a temporary phase of one's life that requires smart work and faith in God to overcome. You won't be poor forever, if you're constantly doing something about building your finances. If things don't happen as planned or you are disappointed by those you trust, do not get depressed or take a deliberate attempt to end your life. You need to be conscious of your mental health and let nothing demoralize you. God created you to be a blessing to others. If it's a situation beyond your control, let go and God will have His way.

Psalm 34:9 (MSG)
"Worship God if you want the best; worship
opens doors to all his goodness."

The Bible in Psalm 61:2 states that when your heart is over-whelmed, God should lead you to the rock that is higher than you. Also, you need to be aware of the state of health of your family and friends. Be conscious of their state of mind and be vigilant. Always be supportive of family and friends, especially when they need it.

Decision Exercise:

....

....

....

....

....

CHAPTER 13

LIVE TODAY LIKE IT'S YOUR LAST

It's certain that a man is to die once. Death is inevitable and there are diverse life expectancy ratios in the world. You have just one life to live. Someday you would leave this world. The question is, "Where are you going afterward?" You don't want to die and open your eyes in hell.

Ephesians 5:5 (GNT)
"You may be sure that no one who is immoral, indecent, or greedy (for greed is a form of idolatry) will ever receive a share in the Kingdom of Christ and of God."

Life is short, irrespective of how long we live. When you leave this world, God is interested in how you lived your life. So many people have lived and died, yet God remains. The living and even the dead talked about God; that's to show that our God is really an everlasting Father and a mighty sovereign.

Romans 6:23 (GNT)
"For sin pays its wage—death, but God's free gift is eternal life in union with Christ Jesus our Lord"

Focus on your soul, that's all that will be left when the flesh dies. Material possessions, wealth, beauty, pleasure and achievements will pass away. Focus and ensure that your soul prospers. That's all God asks of you.

Ecclesiastes 12:6-7 (MSG)
"Life, lovely while it lasts, is soon over. Life as we know it, precious and beautiful, ends. The body

*is put back in the same ground it came from. The
spirit returns to God, who first breathed it."*

Do not boast of anything, especially because you are not certain of tomorrow. If you know the good to do, and you refuse to do it, you err. Life, in a twinkle of an eye, would be over. The end is what is most important. One life to live and soon it would be over. The things of life will pass away and only that which we did for God would count.

James 4:14 (KJV)
*"Whereas ye know not what shall be on the morrow. For
what is your life? It is even a vapour, that appeareth
for a little time, and then vanisheth away."*

Your life now is your legacy. People will talk about your good works when you die. You live and write your story each day you're alive. In life, when you have God, the end always would be greater than the beginning. Give yourself to God, so He can use you and you can die empty. Don't worry about anything, instead appreciate God for the gift of life and don't be scared of the inevitable.

Hebrews 12:14 (KJV)
*"Follow peace with all men, and holiness, without which
no man shall see the Lord: Live your life like you're aware
of when you'll die. Life is full of uncertainties. The way of
holiness is the only way that leads to heaven. Sow goodwill
ahead of you, not curses. God will help us in Jesus' name."*

There are spiritual forces that can make a person die untimely. I pray you shall not be a victim of untimely death because God has promised you a satisfactory long life on the premise of your salvation.

Decision Exercise:

....

....

....

....

CHAPTER 14

Christ, Your Driver

Since Christ died on the cross to redeem us, we must strengthen our faith. Live your life centered on God's will. Love one another as love covers many sins. Hear the Word of God, believe in it, repent from your sin; which is contrary to the will of God, confess your faith in Christ, be baptized in the name of Jesus Christ and receive the gift of the Holy Ghost. Withhold nothing from God, surrender all to Him. Accept Christ as your personal Lord and saviour. For when a just man falls, he shall rise again seven times.

2 Corinthians 5:17 (KJV)
"Therefore if any man be in Christ, he is a new creature: old things are passed away; behold, all things are become new"

Rejuvenate your life in Christ if you have given your life to Him. God is willing and is able to deliver those who trust in Him. Constantly read and meditate on the word of God. Praise and pray fervently. Subject your physical self. Live a Godly life and be dead to your past life. God, in His Word, has told you how to live your life. Do not leave your life to chance.

Deuteronomy 4:29-31 (MSG)
"But even there, if you seek GOD, your God, you'll be able to find him if you're serious, looking for him with your whole heart and soul. When troubles come and all these awful things happen to you, in future days you will come back to GOD, your God, and listen obediently to what he says. GOD,

your God, is above all a compassionate God. In the end, he will not abandon you, he won't bring you to ruin, he won't forget the covenant with your ancestors which he swore to them."

It is not too late to change if you truly want to. God is always ready to extend mercy to anyone who asks. Stop whatever sin that pushes you away from God. Face the consequences as they now are, rather than what they will become; do it for your sake and for those you love.

Romans 3:20-24 (GNT)

"For no one is put right in God's sight by doing what the Law requires; what the Law does is to make us know that we have sinned. But now God's way of putting people right with himself has been revealed. It has nothing to do with law, even though the Law of Moses and the prophets gave their witness to it. God puts people right through their faith in Jesus Christ. God does this to all who believe in Christ, because there is no difference at all: everyone has sinned and is far away from God's saving presence. But by the free gift of God's grace all are put right with him through Christ Jesus, who sets them free."

You are forgiven, gifted, and free. Break free from anything that steals your joy. Do not be found in places where the mercy of God won't be there to save you because God shows mercy to those He chooses to. You need to have a vision to keep you on track, so you can focus on achieving your goals. It's not just obedience to the law that makes us saved but accepting Jesus Christ as Lord and personal saviour.

Titus 2:11-14 (MSG)

"God's readiness to give and forgive is now public. Salvation's available for everyone! We're being shown how to turn our backs on a godless, indulgent life, and how to take on a God-filled, God- honoring life. This new life is starting right now and is whetting our appetites for the glorious day when our great God and Savior, Jesus Christ, appears. He

offered himself as a sacrifice to free us from a dark, rebellious life into this good, pure life, making us a people he can be proud of, energetic in goodness."

Decision Exercise:

....
....
....
....

CHAPTER 15

Prayers

When you worry about a situation, it changes nothing but when you pray about that situation, it changes everything. God is in control and He reigns forever. Prayer is the master key that opens all closed doors. Praying is an act of talking to God. Inasmuch as you need to talk to God through prayers, you also very much need to hear from Him (by reading His word: the Bible). You can't keep talking without listening. There is a dire need to communicate effectively with God and it will benefit you more if you listen and pay attention rather than just talk.

Proverbs 20:27 (MSG)
"GOD is in charge of human life, watching
and examining us inside and out"

Whatsoever your heart desires, pray, believe and you shall receive them. Don't take for granted your daily devotion to God. The devil wants to stop you from fulfilling God's plan for your life but don't let him stop you. God's wish is that you prosper. Talk to God but don't be so desperate for answers. God also wants our prayers to be backed up with righteousness.

James 5:13 (GNT)
"Are any among you in trouble? They should
pray. Are any among you happy?
They should sing praises"

There is power in prayer. It is disastrous to start a day without praying. Humble your heart and go on your knees and commit your life and day into the hands of God.

1 Thessalonians 5:16-18 (KJV)
"Rejoice evermore. Pray without ceasing. In
everything, give thanks: for this is the will
of God in Christ Jesus concerning you".

Whenever you are troubled, pray and sing praises to God. The more you pray, the more you gain power. Believe God is going to do a new thing in your life and whatever seems impossible, God will make possible.

Philippians 4:6-7 (GNT)
"Don't worry about anything, but in all your prayers
ask God for what you need, always asking him
with a thankful heart. And God's peace, which is far
beyond human understanding, will keep your hearts
and minds safe in union with Christ Jesus."

1. Thank you, Lord for the gift of life, provision and protection.

2. Lord, in all the ways that I have sinned against you, forgive me and give me the grace not to go back to my old life.

3. Defend your interests in my life, in Jesus' name.

4. Dear God, give me the grace to wait and trust you.

5. I receive the grace to excel at all times in Jesus' name.

6. Lord, help me to be rightly positioned in your divine favour.

7. Lord, I shall be all you want me to be.

8. Lord, please make known the secrets of my life, so as to make my life better.

9.   God, grant me favour and establish the work of my hands.

10.   Lord, please eliminate from me thoughts that will divert me from your original plan for my life.

11.   The promise of God shall be fulfilled in my life and that of my family!

12.   Lord, give me the strength to be happy in whatever situation I find myself. Give me the grace to understand that my current position is temporary and grant me eternal joy.

13.   Lord, give me the ability not to condition my joy to achievements in this life but to enjoy and appreciate you for the progress in my journey through life.

14.   God, be at the center of my relationships and direct me in all my ways.

15.   Lord, I pray against satanic attacks on my marriage; may it must honour God.

16.   Let my end be better than my beginning.

17.   I shall die empty; I shall excel in life.

18.   I decree that the Joy of the Lord is my strength!

19.   More of you God and less of me in my life's journey.

20.   Thank you Lord, for the answered prayers, in Jesus' name I pray, Amen.

1 Peter 2:4 (GNT)
"Come to the Lord, the living stone rejected
by people as worthless but chosen
by God as valuable".

"Stone Origin is carefully written and packaged for young people. The author addresses the peculiar issues youths are grappling with and posits divine solutions to the major challenges of the day. It is a clarion call to youths to embrace and live by tried and tested divine principles."

Dr D.K Olukoya
General Overseer, MFM Worldwide

ABOUT STONE ORIGIN

The book Stone Origin is a navigational compass for young adults. It emphasizes the possibilities and expectation of challenges for young people while single, in courtship and in marriage as well as lifestyle, career and life principles.
The book then introduces enduring biblical principles that resolve these mysteries in divine values as taught throughout the scriptures and necessary prayers to help us in our journey through life. Life is a journey, and the grace of God coupled with knowing and understanding divine principles is a prerequisite for greatness.

ABOUT THE AUTHOR

Nonyelim Awele Okolie is a Sociology graduate with a Master of Business Administration in view at the University of Lagos. She is a Chartered management professional and served with AIESEC Lagos and the Future Awards Africa. Nonye is currently the COO at Leadspace as well as the Operations Lead at Passion Incubator.In her spiritual engagements, she was the youth secretary, MFM, Akoka Zone. She currently serves with the White Collars Bloc at Eden Centre. She is very passionate about helping people discover ingenious potentials and grow within the prism of biblical-ordained principles.

ISBN 978 - 978 - 973 - 216 - 6